A LADY'S RETURN

SWEET REGENCY ROMANCE

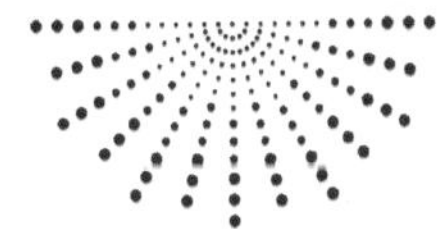

CHARLOTTE DARCY

SWEETBOOKHUB.COM

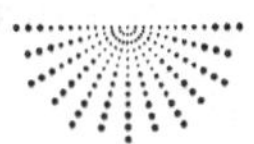

All is fair in love and war, or so they say. But for Caroline Easton, a woman of private means, living quietly in the Berkshire countryside, there had been little fairness in her treatment at cupid's hand thus far. It was late spring, the hedgerows and woodlands bursting with life and all around the village of Brimpton Common, there seemed a freshness in the air and an expectation of the summer to come.

Caroline was on her way to meet with her friend, Anne Harper, a woman with rather more luck in love than she and who was engaged to be married that very month. The two had been friends ever since Caroline had moved to Brimpton Common from

London, finding refuge in its peaceful beauty, after the tempestuous life of the city.

The sweet scent of roses and honeysuckle on the air added a spring to her step. Delighted with the morning, she hummed to herself. At twenty-seven years old, she had become accustomed to spinsterhood and the village was her world. Keeping busy, she was involved in almost every charitable endeavor and an active member of Saint Bartholomew's church. As she passed the church, she paused to call out to the rector who was just emerging after Evensong.

"Good evening to you, Mr. Hickson."

The elderly rector waved. "Good evening to you, Miss Easton. Are you on your way to the manor house?" he asked.

Caroline nodded. "Yes, I must ensure the bride-to-be is in good humor. There is not long to go now," Caroline replied.

"Indeed, do give her my best wishes. The day fast approaches," he called out, giving her another wave as he ambled off across the churchyard.

The manor house lay around half a mile from the center of the village, along a driveway lined with yew trees. It was a familiar walk for Caroline, for she and Anne often took tea together or would dine at one another's homes. Caroline could not be happier for her friend, who was marrying Sir Percy Lindorp, a man of means who was rumored to be worth £6000 a year and had an estate two villages over at Petworth.

Caroline smiled, she had little interest in marriage and rarely gave it a second thought. Her own inheritance had been substantial and she was happy in her home at Brimpton Grange, a fine house on the opposite side of the village. There, she lived comfortably with her faithful maid, Susan, and a daily cook named Mrs. Duggs, who, between them, saw to her every need. Life was happy for Caroline and she spent her days at leisure or engaged in the good works for which she was so highly regarded.

The manor house was a sprawling, ivy-clad, old place, belonging to Anne's father, Lord Brimpton. It had been in the family for generations and was without a doubt the finest house in the village. Caroline knocked at the large and imposing oak door, looking up at the window directly above which Anne used as a drawing room.

Sure enough, a moment later, Anne's face appeared at the window and she smiled, waving enthusiastically. The window was pulled up and Anne leaned out, her long dark, curly hair falling down around her face, as she called out to Caroline below.

"You took your time, it is nearly six o'clock," she said.

"I was so absorbed in my book that I quite lost track of the time and I had to call upon Mrs. Wilkes to discuss the flowers for the guild benefit next week," Caroline called up.

Anne laughed. "You and your good works. Come on up, we shall have tea. I have such a lot to tell you," Anne replied, just as the door was opened by the maid.

"Good day, ma'am," she said, curtseying to Caroline and ushering her inside.

"Thank you, Helen," Caroline replied, stepping over the threshold.

The hallway was dark and cool after the bright warmth of the day outside and Caroline removed her bonnet, her own hair now falling down her back. She caught a glimpse of herself in a mirror by the door and quickly straightened her hair. She was blonde, her long hair her pride and joy. Thought by many to be a pretty woman, with deep blue eyes and a dimple in her chin, she was pleased with her appearance. In her time, she had attracted the attention of many a man in Brimpton Common, but no one had caught her attention enough for her to show an interest in reciprocation. Caroline was happy as she was and needed no intrusion on her comfortable and peaceful existence.

"Do not dally in the hallway, Caroline, come and join me. We shall have tea, Helen, thank you," Anne called out from the landing above, beckoning Caroline to follow her.

Caroline smiled. Anne always was enthusiastic about her visits, and she hurried up the stairs, following her friend into the comfortably furnished drawing room.

"You are ever so excitable today," Caroline said, and her friend laughed.

"You would be too if your wedding dress had arrived

from London *this very day,*" she said, pointing to a very large box on the table by the window.

It was done up in a bow that Anne now proceeded to ceremoniously undo with a flourish.

"You have waited for me? Oh, Anne, I am sorry. I would have come sooner had I known," Caroline said.

Anne shook her head. "I wanted you to see it. As you know, I went up to London a month ago for the fitting but now the dress is here. What do you think?" she asked, pulling the dress out from the box.

It was exquisite and Caroline could not help but smile, as Anne held it up to herself and twirled about the room. It was made of a beautiful peach colored fabric, with lacy cuffs and a trim about the neck. It really was a most fitting wedding dress and Caroline knew her friend would look ever so pretty when she wore it.

"Do say you like it," Anne said.

Caroline laughed. "Of course, I like it, it is beautiful, Anne," she replied, and her friend breathed a sigh of relief.

"I did wonder," she said, laying the dress back in its box.

"Whatever for? You will be the prettiest bride that Brimpton Common has ever seen."

"I am so nervous about the wedding. That was why I was so longing to see you today, you are the only person I can speak to about such things," Anne replied, coming to sit opposite Caroline, just as the maid brought in the tea.

"Nervous? Why? You have nothing to be nervous about. Percy is the sweetest of gentlemen and he loves you beyond words," Caroline replied, taking a sip of tea.

"But I feel so inadequate. He is so good and kind and sweet, just as you say. But I must confess I feel so plain and unworthy at times." She shook her head and there was a hint of moisture in her eyes.

"It is just nerves, Anne. It will pass," Caroline replied reaching over and squeezing her friend's hand.

"But the wedding is so near at hand and so much depends upon it. What if I am being a fool?"

Caroline only laughed. "You would not be the first bride to suffer such nerves, and neither will you be the last. We have all experienced heartache over a man," she said.

Anne looked up at her in surprise. "But you have not. You have never known such a state of mind, Caroline," she said.

Caroline sighed. It had been a slip of the tongue to make mention of her own past, a past she would rather have forgotten. In Brimpton Common she was known as a charitable spinster, an attractive woman, but one for whom romance was of no consequence. Yet it had not always been the case that Caroline had refused the attentions of gentlemen and now, with Anne looking at her curiously, she felt obliged to offer an explanation.

"Well, if you must know, I was once engaged to be married," she replied.

Anne gasped. "But I never knew," she said, as though it were her right to have done so.

"We all of us have things we wish to keep from others. I tell no one of it and I would rather it were left in the past where it belongs," she replied.

"Oh, come now, Caroline. You cannot simply tell me half a story when the subject matter is of such great importance. Who was this man? And more importantly what happened to him? Why are you not married now? Was there a scandal?" Anne asked, waiting with bated breath for Caroline's response.

"Goodness me, Anne, what questions. Very well, I shall tell you the story but it must go no further than your drawing room. As I say, the past is in the past and it's best that it was left there," Caroline replied.

"Certainly, the secret will be safe with me," Anne replied, though Caroline knew that to her detriment, Anne was not the sort of woman who could easily keep a confidence.

"I was barely a woman when it occurred, only eighteen years of age. This was back in London at the beginning of my first season. I was young and naïve. There was a ball, given by Lord and Lady Somerfield of Greenwich. My mother allowed me to go with a cousin acting as a chaperone. Well, it was there that I met the Duke of Norcroft, Louis Howard. A charming and dashing young man of twenty-one and who quite swept me off my feet. We danced and he told me I was beautiful," Caroline said, sighing at the long-repressed memory of that fateful night.

"Yes, and then what happened? He proposed to you immediately I suppose?" Anne said, hanging on Caroline's every word.

"Not immediately, no," Caroline replied, rolling her eyes at Anne's overt romanticism. "We met several times more. In London, there is no end of opportunity for social gathering, and our paths crossed at balls and soirees across the town. Eventually, he stole a kiss, one which I regret I reciprocated and even enjoyed. I was entirely taken in by him and believed that he would ask for my hand in marriage. I made it known to my mother and father that I would agree to such a proposal for it was the most perfect match."

"You would have been a duchess," Anne said, her excitement seeming to build with every word Caroline uttered.

"I would have been a duchess, yes, and I allowed such thoughts to run away with me. A foolish thing indeed," Caroline replied.

"But what happened? Why are you not married now?" Anne asked.

Caroline sighed. It pained her to think back on the past, for her life was so happy now, despite the heartbreak she had endured at the hands of the Duke of Norcroft.

"He changed. It was all of a sudden. I was due to meet him at a party given by the Earl and Countess of Coburn but he never arrived. I sent word to his residence and received no reply, I even called upon him, as humiliating as that may sound. But there was no response, simply nothing. He froze me out and broke off all communication," Caroline replied.

"The swine," Anne hissed, a tear welling up in her eye, as though it were she and not Caroline who had been so wronged.

"There is more too, for I discovered shortly afterward that he was engaged to another. One, Victoria Bartlett, Lady Victoria Bartlett, the daughter of Lord Bartlett of Grisham. It was a terrible blow, Anne, and one I do not wish to be reminded of."

"No, indeed, but have you seen him again?" she

asked, ignoring Caroline's dictum that the conversation was at an end.

"No, and I have no wish to do so. He no doubt resides at his estate and at his home in town. I am sure he and the Duchess are very happy together. It was after that unfortunate incident that I withdrew and when my parents died, I decided to leave town and move to the countryside and the rest you know," Caroline replied, finishing her tea.

"Quite remarkable. The man is a swine, I shall say it again," Anne said, brushing the tear from her eye and rising to her feet.

"Well, it is in the past now, Anne, and I would prefer for its memory to remain there," Caroline said.

"But not all men are like this wicked rake," Anne replied.

"No, but when one has been hurt once it becomes increasingly harder to trust again," Caroline replied.

She had often told herself much the same, but she knew that however hard she tried she would be forever haunted by that sad and painful experience in the prime of her youth. It was not that she had no wish for marriage but she was scared that her heart could not bear to be broken again. Instead, she kept it guarded and allowed only those she could entirely trust to enter in. There was no place there for a man, not if he was to turn out to be precisely the same as Louis and lead her again into hope then dashed to pieces in disappointment and anguish.

"I am sorry if I upset you," Anne said when Caroline came to leave a little later on.

"You did not upset me, Anne. But I would rather think of you and your happiness than dwell in the past. I am sorry you did not know of my previous engagement. Though it was hardly an engagement such as you now enjoy, and I would rather forget it," Caroline said, kissing her friend goodbye.

It was a beautiful spring evening outside, the shadows growing long, as the sun sank below the horizon. As Caroline walked home, she thought back to her conversation with Anne. Should she have been more revelatory about her past in years gone by? She and Anne had known one another ever since Caroline had arrived in Brimpton Common, and yet she had never told her of this sad fact from her past.

Why should I have done? she reasoned to herself, *it is in the past and the past is another country.*

But the resurfacing of those memories had brought with it a sense of sorrow once again. Caroline had tried so hard to suppress her feelings and to forget all about the Duke of Norcroft. But try as she might, and despite all the sorrow and heartache he had caused her, she still felt something for him. Perhaps it was the naivete of youth which had made her fall in love... yet now her heart still betrayed her, as she wondered again what might have been.

She had never known the reason why he had broken off with her, nor why he had taken up with another woman. He had spoken so often of his tenderness for her, of his deep feelings and love. It had come as the most tragic of blows to know his rejection. For a long time, she had been angry with him and spoke his name to her mother and father as mud. But, as the years had gone by, she had realized with sadness, that she still loved him and that whatever man might come after him could never truly match the Duke as a man to capture her heart.

You must put him out of your mind, she told herself, as she arrived home that evening.

But try as she might, the memories had been awakened and Caroline knew that the feelings she harbored for Louis would be difficult to rid herself of. Was she doomed to be ever trapped by her past, or could there ever be hope for a better future?

CHAPTER TWO

Caroline returned from a meeting of the Brimpton Common Lady's Guild, a charitable endeavor that sought to send relief to the poorer parts of the capital. It had been a good morning, spent sorting out donations of clothes. Lady Brimpton, in her capacity as chair lady, had given a speech on the importance of philanthropy. Caroline and Anne had sat together and with only a few weeks to go before the wedding their talk had been of only one topic.

Caroline was grateful that Anne, uncharacteristically, had adhered to her wishes. There was no further mention of the Duke of Norcroft nor of Caroline's matrimonial state. With great effort, she had pushed aside the thoughts of Louis and had concentrated instead upon her charitable work. That afternoon, she was due at the rectory to discuss the arrangements for a children's tea to be given in the village on the last Saturday in June. She had returned home for a brief luncheon before stepping out again.

"Please, ma'am, a letter has arrived for you," Susan said, as Caroline entered the house.

"Oh, thank you, Susan, would you bring it to me in the dining room?" Caroline replied.

The maid nodded. "Mrs. Duggs has left a tureen of soup and fresh bread there for you," she said.

The house was large, though not overbearing and surrounded by mature grounds which were kept for Caroline by a gardener, Mr. Edwards. She could see him now out of the dining room window, clipping at the box hedge which surrounded the rose garden. It was a beautiful view, the roses in bloom. Grateful for her blessings, she helped herself to soup from the tureen on the sideboard, just as Susan brought in the letter.

"Just there, thank you, Susan," Caroline said, and the maid laid it down on the table.

It was rare for her to receive letters but she recognized the handwriting on the envelope immediately. It was from her uncle, Richard Easton, and was no doubt a missive reminding her of all she had lost in moving to the countryside. He was her only surviving relative and took any opportunity to extol the virtues of London life over that of her own. He had visited her once in Brimpton Common, declaring it to be a provincial backwater, a place so quiet that it drove him to distraction. She smiled to herself, eating her soup, a most excellent bisque, before opening the letter and beginning to read.

"Oh, goodness me," she cried, reading the letter through again.

It was not the usual mix of gossip and gentle chastisement which her uncle specialized in. Instead, the letter told of his sudden illness and that he had taken to his bed with a fever some two days before. It was, he thought, far from life-threatening, but he dearly desired the comfort of his favorite, and only, niece at his bedside.

Caroline rang the little bell on the table.

Susan appeared a moment later, holding a plate of cakes in her hand. "A little something sweet, ma'am?" she asked.

Caroline shook her head. "No, Susan. The letter was from my uncle, he has taken ill. I must leave for London at once. Would you tell Mr. Edwards to run to the village and summon a carriage for me? I am sure young Samuel Timpson would be willing to drive. It is of the utmost importance that I leave at once," Caroline said.

Susan curtsied. "Of course, ma'am. I shall see to it at once." Looking worried, she hurried out of the room.

A feeling of dread, like a heavy weight settle in Caroline's stomach. Susan would pack a bag, in readiness for her journey, so there was little to do but to pace before the window.

He writes that it is a minor ailment, but he would not command my presence if it were not a serious matter, she thought to herself, as she paced up and down. How time could drag when the matter at hand was urgent.

Around an hour later, Caroline found herself in the carriage departing Brimpton Common for London. She had left a note for Anne and instructions for Susan and Mrs. Duggs as to the arrangements for her charitable work.

"And send a note to the rectory; I am afraid the arrangements for the children's tea will have to wait," she had said, as the two servants waved her off.

Now, she sat back in the carriage as Samuel Timpson made no sparing of the horses. Even so, it would be late that evening before she arrived in London. How she hoped that time would fly. She loved her uncle dearly and if he was ill, then Caroline's place was at his side.

I only hope it is not serious, she thought, as the carriage sped along the country lanes and she wondered just what the next few days would bring.

I t was dusk by the time they arrived in the quiet streets of the capital. Caroline's uncle lived close to the newly conceived Regent's Park, on a wide avenue of attractive townhouses. He had lived there for the past five years, often declaring in his letters that he liked to be at the center of things and boasting of the many parties and soirees he attended with the great and the good of the city.

A solitary light was burning in an upstairs window. Caroline paid Samuel Timpson generously and thanked him for the swiftness of their travel. A blush crossed his pale face, making the freckles stand out in the gloom. He would return to the village that night and she would send for him when she wished to return.

"Goodnight, ma'am," he said, as he placed her bag on the top step by the front door of the house.

"Goodnight, Samuel, and take care as you return," she said, waving him off.

The door was answered by her uncle's valet, Perkins, a tall man with a squint, who welcomed her inside with grateful relief.

"Your uncle has been intolerable, Miss Easton. Quite intolerable since all this began," he whispered.

"He was never one for taking to his sickbed. That is why I came at once," she replied.

"The gout, ma'am. That is how it began, but he now has a fever, one which makes him ever so demanding," Perkins replied, rolling his eyes.

"More demanding than usual?" Caroline asked.

The valet merely nodded his head.

"He would see you immediately, ma'am, I am sure," Perkins said, leading her upstairs to her uncle's sitting room.

She found Richard with his feet propped up by the fire. Despite the warmth of the late spring evening, it was blazing with a fresh log and the room felt uncomfortably warm. Her uncle was a small man and he appeared even smaller, hunched over in his chair, and wrapped in blankets. His face lit up when Perkins announced Caroline's arrival and he called her in with a smile on his lips and a twinkle in his eye.

"My dearest niece, how wonderful to see you. You must have come at once, for I only posted the letter yesterday morning," he said, and she crossed the room to kiss him on the cheek.

"Of course, I came at once, Uncle. Your condition

demanded it," she replied, sitting down in the chair opposite.

"You are very kind, my favorite niece," he said, causing her to laugh.

"Your only niece, Uncle, and I shall remain here until you are better," she said.

"Or I am dead," he replied, gloomily.

"Perkins tells me it is your gout which afflicts you and now a fever. It is hardly the summoning of death," she said.

Richard laughed. "Perhaps, but whether death awaits me or not I am so very glad to have a visit from my dear country niece."

"It is an odd feeling to be back in London," she said, for Caroline avoided the capital as much as possible, preferring the countryside and its quiet ways to the hustle and bustle of town.

"A visit far too delayed. But whilst you are here you must make good use of your time. Knowing you are close at hand is tonic enough for me. Do not feel that you must remain at my side all the time. I shall call for you if I feel the end is near," he said.

"Your dramatic inclinations know no bounds. I shall avail myself of the opportunities afforded me here," she replied.

"You must, I am glad to hear it, my dear. Now, I think it is high time you had a little supper and took to your bed. You do not need to remain politely talking to me," he said, ringing the bell for Perkins.

"I am quite happy to remain politely talking to you," she replied, but he would hear none of it, and Perkins was instructed to take Caroline to her chambers and see to it that she was served a simple yet adequate supper.

"Then I shall see you in the morning," she replied, and Richard bid her goodnight.

Upstairs, Caroline found herself yawning and was grateful to her uncle for suggesting an early retirement. She ate her supper and readied herself for bed, pausing to glance out of the window across the park and city beyond. It held so many memories, some good and some bad. She had mixed feelings about returning there, though to be with her uncle was of the most importance.

And when he is better I shall return to Brimpton

Common, she thought to herself, climbing into bed and snuffing out her candle. As the darkness surrounded her, her thoughts turned to Anne's wedding and she fell into a deep and dreamless sleep.

~

The next morning dawned bright and early, Caroline rose before the maid had brought her hot water and towels and she was already dressed, as a knock came at the door.

"Come in," she called out.

The maid appeared with a look of surprise on her face. "I am sorry, ma'am, I would have come earlier if I had known," she said.

Caroline smiled. "I am quite capable of making my own arrangements, thank you. Is my uncle awake?" she asked.

The maid nodded putting down the towels. "Oh, yes, ma'am. Mr. Easton has been awake for hours. He is at his breakfast," she replied.

Caroline made her way downstairs and she found

her uncle in the same position as she had left him the evening before. He was eating bread and jam, a cup of tea at his side and a book open on his knees.

"Ah, Caroline, my dear. I feel in good humor this morning, it must be your arrival which has done it," he said, beckoning her to sit opposite him.

"No longer on the point of death?" she asked, smiling at him.

With a wink, he shook his head. "I think death has passed over us like the Exodus."

"You are incorrigible, Uncle. I think you have merely summoned me here under false pretenses. You know I dislike coming up to town," she said.

"But you love to see your uncle and you have not done so for some time," he said, as the maid brought in a tray of breakfast things for Caroline.

"Thank you, Lucy. We shall dine on our knees this morning," Richard said.

The maid curtsied. "As you wish, sir. Am I to make the same arrangements for luncheon?" she asked.

He nodded. "Why not? I am sending my niece out

on an errand for me this morning," he said, grinning at Caroline, who rolled her eyes.

"Another ploy to force me from the house. And what errand am I to run for you?" she asked.

"I want you to go to Mr. Hatchard's bookshop on Piccadilly. He will have a volume of poetry there for me. I sent Perkins to order it some days ago. Would you collect it for me?"

Caroline nodded. "Yes, Uncle, I will," she replied, and foregoing her breakfast, she put on her bonnet and stepped out into the pleasant, early spring morning.

The streets were already busy and despite her misgivings about being back in the capital, Caroline was pleased for the fresh air and walk. She felt stiff after sitting in the bumpy carriage for much of yesterday afternoon and the walk to Piccadilly did her good. Much had changed in the capital since last she was there, but she recognized many of the shops as she went along, pausing at times to look into the windows and marvel at the latest fashions and goods for sale.

Quite unlike our little shop in Brimpton Common,

she thought to herself, pausing to gaze at a dress in the window of a millinery shop, a short distance from her destination.

She was examining the dress when she felt a presence behind her and saw the reflection of a gentleman in the glass. He was looking at her intently and she could feel his eyes on the back of her head. The reflection startled her, the tall top hat reminding her of ... but it could not be. She turned, and to her amazement, she found none other than the Duke of Norcroft staring back at her. The sight of him caused her to exclaim in surprise and he took a step back, as though equally startled by her presence.

"Well now, this is a most unexpected pleasure," he said, a look of abject amazement coming over his face.

"I did not expect to see you either," she said, drawing herself up and recovering something of her demeanor.

What was he doing there? And what now should she do? For a moment, she thought of fleeing, the memories of the past flooded back almost dropping her to her knees. But why should she run? She had as much right as he to be on Piccadilly that morning.

"Are you well?" he asked.

Caroline grimaced, knowing that her response would determine much of what the Duke's next move might be.

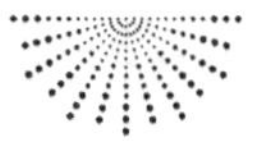

"I am well, thank you," she replied, deciding that a curt but polite response was in order and would hopefully see an end to their meeting as soon as possible.

Anger, betrayal, hurt, sadness, and more coursed through her. The memories that Anne had aroused were enough to disturb her peaceful and tranquil world. Now, faced with the man himself, she felt her feelings turned entirely upon their head. The urge to run away was strong. To flee, to never see him again, for she had not wished to see him in the first place. Yet, a part of her was intrigued by his presence and she wondered if she dared demand an explanation for his treatment of her all those years ago.

"That is good to hear. What a strange coincidence that we should meet like this," he continued, as a smile played across his face.

The years had been kind to him and he had grown from the handsome look of youth into the handsome look of a man. Through his tailored jacket, she could see that he was well built, athletic even, his dark brown hair was combed neatly to the side. But it was his eyes that Caroline remembered the most. They were wide, hazel in color, and gave her their full attention, as they stood outside the millinery shop.

"It is," she replied, embarrassed by his fixed gaze so much that she looked down at her feet.

It annoyed her that her hands were trembling and her heart was racing like a runaway horse. She thought she had pushed aside her feelings towards the Duke, even the anger she felt at what he had done to her. But even now, faced with him again, she felt an overwhelming sense of those old and familiar feelings returning. He still possessed that charm and attraction which had so allured her in her youth. She wanted desperately to know the reasons for his betrayal and at the same time, she was desperate to flee from his side as soon as possible.

"You look ever so well. The country air must be doing you good," he said.

Swallowing down a lump of fear, she nodded. "It suits me very well," she managed.

"But tell me, how have you been?" he asked, a question which she found it hard to respond without being impolite.

It was he who had left her! It was he who had broken her heart by his betrayal and it was he who had not replied to her letters begging him to reconsider. He had married another woman and left her to be a spinster, alone and forgotten. How dare he now enquire as to how she had been in the years which intervened between their final meeting and this.

"I have kept myself busy with charitable works in the village of Brimpton Common, where I live a comfortable life," she said, hoping that her response would suffice.

"Ah, yes, I heard you had moved out into the darkest countryside, never to be seen again," he said, laughing.

"It is preferable to the town, I find," she said.

Slowly, he shook his head. "Really? I find my estate to be the dullest of places. I spend more and more time in town these days," he said, still blocking her path towards Mr. Hatchard's bookshop.

Caroline wondered what had become of his wife. She took no periodicals in Brimpton Common, nor did she read the society pages. The gossip and intrigues of the aristocracy did not interest her one bit, she preferred to devote her time to good causes rather than delighting in the downfall or not of others.

"I see, well, it has been... pleasant to see you again, Your Grace. I must be getting along now, I have an errand to run for my uncle, and he will be expecting me for luncheon." Caroline stepped around the Duke hoping this was the end of it.

Much to her desolation, he followed her towards the bookshop.

"Ah, yes, your uncle. Is he well? I have occasionally seen him at social gatherings, though we move in quite different circles. I trust he is keeping well?" the Duke asked.

Caroline turned to him with a look of annoyance on

her face. "If you must know, he is rather suffering at the moment. His gout is playing up and he has a fever. That is why I have come from 'the darkest countryside,' as you so eloquently put it. I shall nurse him back to health and then return to Berkshire. I have little desire to remain in town a moment longer than I have to," Caroline said, pausing now outside Mr. Hatchard's bookshop, as the Duke blocked her path once more.

"I am terribly sorry to hear that. My grandfather suffered terribly with gout and I know it to be a most abominable affliction. There is no pain like it, or so they say. I myself have not had the misfortune to succumb to it but coupled with a fever it must be unbearable. Do send him my best wishes," Louis said.

Caroline nodded. "I will do. Now, if you will excuse me, I must be getting on."

The Duke remained persistent. "But you yourself are well?" he asked, as they stood blocking the door to the bookshop.

"Your Grace, may I ask why my health or the health

of my uncle are of any concern to you?" Caroline asked, fixing him with a hard stare.

At these words, his face fell and he seemed almost hurt by what she had said. He stepped back, biting his lip, as though considering his next move, before looking up at her and furrowing his brow.

"I was merely hoping that... well, this happy coincidence might be a sign to us. A sign that we should meet again. How long are you in town for?" he asked.

Caroline shook her head. Despite her curiosity and the questions she still wanted to ask, she knew that her heart could take no further emotional torment. She had no desire to prolong the feelings which were already arising within her and wanted to part from his company as soon as possible.

"I do not know why you even care, given everything which has transpired between us. I think it for the best if we bid one another a good day. I shall be in town for as long as it takes to see my uncle well again. That is all. Now, if you will excuse me, I must collect my uncle's book," she said, stepping past him into the bookshop.

"But Caroline, I was only..." he began, but she roundly ignored him, making for the counter and calling for assistance.

"I have a book to collect for my uncle, Mr. Richard Easton," she said, and the assistant went off to find it.

She could see the Duke hovering outside the shop and made a point of lingering there far longer than she had intended. *Why was he suddenly so interested in her and her welfare?* It seemed so bizarre. She had not heard anything from him since that last day they had met for a walk in the park and he had told her again how much he loved her. She had parted from his company that day with a heart as light as a feather, her joy knowing no bounds. But in only a week those feelings had been shattered like a china doll and she had descended to the depths of abject misery and all for the sake of the Duke of Norcroft. Well, she was not going to make the same mistake again and thanking the assistant for his help she tucked her uncle's book into a bag and left the shop.

"Will you not hear me, Caroline?" the Duke asked, springing out on her, as she turned to cross the park.

"No, I will not," she replied, turning to him angrily.

"Please, Caroline, I..." he began, but she had no desire to hear him.

"We have nothing more to say to one another, Louis. You had your chance to make an explanation many years ago. Do not think that simply because we meet by chance in Piccadilly that you have the right to command my attention as you seem to think. I want nothing more to do with you," she said, feeling magnanimous in her position.

She had felt so powerless in his betrayal. Her letters had gone unanswered, her calling card returned and she had received no explanation for the heartbreak he had rendered unto her. But now, the power lay with her and she delighted in dismissing him, as she hurried across the park.

When she had gone a safe distance, she looked back. He was still standing at the other end of the long avenue of trees which led towards her uncle's house. He looked imploringly at her, as though wondering whether or not to pursue her. But in response, she tossed her head, and walked on, hoping that she would never see the Duke again.

And good riddance to him, she thought to herself, as

she let herself into her uncle's house, *I hope I never see him again.*

CHAPTER FOUR

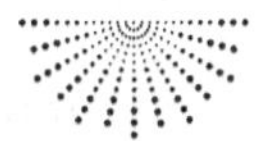

*L*ouis stood despondently staring at Caroline's figure, retreating along the tree-lined avenue across the park. He had been so delighted to chance upon her outside the millinery shop on Piccadilly. It had seemed fated, as though her presence were a sign that something of the past could still be rescued.

But I can hardly blame her for her reaction towards me, I behaved so appallingly, he thought to himself turning with a sigh and wandering off towards home.

He had thought often of Caroline in the years which had passed and had kept a discreet eye upon her whereabouts and social engagements. He had found it quite unbelievable that she had not taken a husband or found herself involved in a romantic tryst. She was as beautiful as he remembered and she seemed entirely wasted upon the little village of Brimpton Common and the charitable works she undertook there.

Since parting from her company all those years ago his own life had been something of a disappointment and his only refuge was the social life he enjoyed here in London. He had come up to town in order to escape the dullness of the countryside and seeing Caroline had sparked a hundred memories in his mind, most notably of the happiness she had brought him.

But I was naïve to think that a few simple words could charm her back into my affections, he told himself, as he approached home.

His house was a fine townhouse, built over four floors and with an imposing black front door. It was there that he entertained many a gathering of the great and good. He was a congenial host and one who often had visitors call upon him. As he approached the house, he saw the carriage of his closest friend, Martin Sewell, standing outside. He was not expecting a caller, for it was almost lunchtime. But the company would be a distraction from his thoughts, which were entirely directed towards Caroline.

How he wished she had allowed him to explain and offer his own description of the sad events which had befallen them. He had felt such guilt in his rejection of her, but her social standing had made it impossible for him to marry her. She had no title and whilst her parents were wealthy, they did not possess the necessary qualities which made their daughter suitable for the title of Duchess. But, in the years which followed, Louis had come to see beyond such things and he was no longer bound by the social mores of expectation placed upon him.

I would have married her, he said to himself.

He climbed the steps to the house, his mind filled with thoughts of Caroline's beauty. A beauty which seemed only to have increased as the years had gone by. Inside, he found Martin's calling card on a silver tray by the aspidistra and called to his butler for drinks to be brought to the drawing room.

"Is he in there, Challoner?" Louis asked, and the butler nodded.

"I showed him in, Your Grace, he has already had a brandy and helped himself to your snuff," the butler replied.

Louis rolled his eyes. "That does not surprise me, Challoner," he replied, making his way across the hallway to the drawing room.

There he found his friend in the middle of extracting snuff from his best ivory snuff box, sneezing, as Louis opened the door.

"Ah, Louis, I was thinking you would never return," Martin said, laying aside the box and coming to shake the Duke's hand.

Martin was a portly gentleman, only a year or so older than Louis himself, with a round red face and whiskers. He was a shipbuilder and joint owner of the firm Sewell & Sewell, whose office stood at Greenwich, though it was his father rather than he who did much of the work. Martin was a man of learning, often buried in books and charts, with little practical head for business. Still, he was a rich man and a loyal friend to Louis, whose friend he had been since school.

"But you helped yourself to brandy and snuff in the

meantime," Louis said, smiling and shaking his head.

"Only the essentials, but I shall stay to luncheon too if you insist," Martin said, sitting down, as Mr. Challoner brought in a tray of drinks.

"I am not terribly hungry, I must confess," Louis said, grateful for the company though feeling in little mood to be sociable.

"Not hungry? But you always have the best of appetites, Louis," Martin said, looking at his friend with a puzzled expression.

"Not today, old friend," Louis replied, taking a drink of brandy and staring vacantly off into the distance.

"Now, come along. That is not your usual attitude; what is wrong? Has something ailed you on your walk? You appear entirely out of humor today... Come now, do tell me, what is wrong?"

Louis shook his head. "It is nothing, only a ghost from the past, that is all."

"You cannot just leave me full of questions like that. I must know what is wrong with you. How can I provide my usual friendly advice to you if I do not know the situation fully?" Martin said.

Louis sighed. "Do you remember Caroline Easton?" Louis asked.

Martin let out an exclamation. "Remember her? Of course, I remember. A more beautiful and vivacious young lady than one could ever possibly hope to meet. She turned heads during her season and you were foolish enough to let her go," Martin said, narrowing his eyes.

"Well, this morning, during my walk along Piccadilly, I chanced upon her outside Mr. Hatchard's bookshop. The lady has returned to town to take care of her uncle who is ill with a fever. You will remember Richard Easton, I suppose?" Louis said.

Martin nodded. "My father had business dealings with him, yes. Did you speak to her? What was her reaction to you?" Martin asked.

"Entirely as I should have expected it to be... but entirely as I wished it not to be," Louis replied.

"You can hardly blame her. Did she give you the old cold shoulder?" Martin asked, laughing.

Louis frowned at him and Martin fell silent.

"She told me that it would be best if the two of us did not see one another again and I received the distinct impression that she wished we had not seen one another today, either," Louis replied.

His mind seemed entirely preoccupied with Caroline, who appeared to him as vividly as though she had been stood immediately before him. He had never truly stopped loving her, though he had known such a thing to be foolish and rash. From the moment he had first set eyes upon her he had been in love and his naivete had been his downfall. His father had forbidden him from marrying her and despite an appeal to his mother she too had cast doubt upon the union. There was to be no marriage of happiness but rather one of duty and it was to Lady Victoria Bartlett that his hand was given, rather than the woman he truly loved.

"But surely, it is fate that has brought you together today. You would never have known her to be present in town had you not chanced upon her. You cannot simply allow her to slip through your fingers in such a manner," Martin said.

"But she grew angry and she has every right to be so. I treated her in such an appalling manner all those years ago," Louis said, shaking his head and taking another drink.

"Then now is the time to make amends. If she is in town for some time then you have the perfect opportunity. Did she not move to some provincial backwater in the wake of your ending the courtship?" Martin asked.

"If you call Berkshire a provincial backwater. I do not understand her attraction to the countryside. We could be the happiest of people," Louis said, though he knew his complaints were a fantasy.

Caroline would never agree to take up their courtship once more even though Louis' current circumstances permitted it.

"You could have been many years ago. Instead, you chose to marry Victoria and what a sorry mess that was," Martin said, shaking his head.

"Yes, indeed," Louis replied, shaking his head.

His marriage to Lady Victoria Bartlett had been a disaster from the very beginning. She had been a philanderer and a woman of the lowest morals. Her dalliances with a string of men had led to her downfall and she had found herself in debt, pursued to London by one of her lovers, whilst Louis had been abroad.

Her pursuer had been a ruthless man by the name of Count Giovanni Battisto, an Italian with a fiery heart and who had taken her life, rather than see her escape from his clutches. Louis had returned to London to find his wife dead and the Count long disappeared. It had been a scandal of the highest order, though mercifully hushed up before too much disaster could come of it.

Louis had found himself a widower and a bachelor once again, having never known the true happiness of marriage. Victoria had been no wife at all and how fortunate it was that she had not born him children, for they too would have suffered dreadfully at her hands. Louis had thought himself to be the recipient of divine retribution for his treatment of Caroline, for had he married her instead of Victoria then much sorrow could have been avoided. But it seemed now that all was lost and he slumped down dejectedly in his chair, desiring only another drink to satiate his woes.

"The years pass, Louis. One cannot hold a grudge

forever, of that I am certain. I have no doubt that she was angry at seeing you so suddenly, but allow her a few days and perhaps you shall find an opportunity again to speak with her. She does not know the full fact of what transpired and why you were forced to seek the hand of a woman other than her. It was not your fault... you must not entirely blame yourself," Martin said, rising from his place to pour another drink.

"I can hardly blame her for being angry, Martin. She has every right to be. I offered her no explanation, nor did I seek to make amends after Victoria's death," Louis replied.

"But you were hardly in a fit state to think of romance at a time like that. Your wife was the cause of the utmost scandal. She did not love you, nor care for you, and it is only through the goodwill of so many that your name did not become a byword for scandal. Thank goodness the whole affair was hushed up. But if you ever sought to marry again then I fear that the knowledge of Victoria's indiscretion would erupt again, this time with far more force than before," Martin said.

"But what would you have me do?" Louis asked, thinking the situation to be entirely unsalvageable.

"I would have you speak with her and make her understand the foolishness of bearing a grudge," Martin replied.

It seemed so simple when he said it, as though Louis could go at once to the home of Richard Easton and request an audience with the woman whose heart he had broken.

"And if she will not listen, as she did not listen today?" Louis asked.

"Today was a shock for you both. When you left home this morning you did not expect to see the woman you once loved, perhaps still love, in Piccadilly. Likewise, as Caroline made her way to Mr. Hatchard's bookshop she too did not expect to meet the man who so ill-treated her all those years ago," Martin replied.

"You hardly paint me in a good light," Louis said, sighing.

"I merely present the facts and tell you that it would be folly if you did not at least try and speak with her on equal terms. Explain what happened, make her understand. A lot of water has passed under the bridge and perhaps now you will find her more amenable," Martin replied.

"Amenable? She fair chased me away and told me we should never see one another again," Louis replied.

"It is a woman's prerogative to behave thus. Ah, now, do I hear the gong for luncheon?" Martin said, finishing his drink and rising from his place.

The summons for luncheon had indeed just sounded. Louis followed his friend to the dining room, where a light collation was awaiting them. But he did not feel like eating nor drinking; he was restless, wondering what to do. Could he really seek out Caroline again? He had behaved so appallingly in the flush of youth, thinking that by ignoring her he could forget the love which lay deep in his heart and move on with his life as the husband of Victoria.

But life had twisted its cruel knife into him and left him bereft. How often, in those dark days when Victoria was still alive, had he wished for things to have been different. He had realized early on that Victoria was not the woman he had hoped for.

Instead, she was a woman who had no love for him and no intention of behaving as his wife. He had spent so many nights in agony over the thought of Caroline, wishing for the day when he might make amends.

But now that that day had come, he felt terrified by the prospect. It had been so sudden and crashed in upon his world with such ferocity as to entirely take him aback. He had not known what to say on Piccadilly that morning, except a simple greeting and the hope that she was well. Yet it was clear he had overstepped the mark and caused her more distress than he would ever have wished. He felt a fool toying with his luncheon, as Martin tucked in hungrily.

"I will have no peace unless I speak with her," he said, voicing his thoughts.

"You will not, my friend," Martin said, slicing vigorously into a piece of boiled tongue.

"Perhaps I could call upon her under some pretense," he replied, scratching his head.

Martin only laughed. "And what possible pretense could there be? You must simply call upon her and ask to speak with her. Then you shall see the true lay of the land. This piccalilli is excellent," Martin said, helping himself from the dish in the center of the table.

Louis pushed his food around his plate, mulling over the decision which now presented itself as an inevitability. To call upon Caroline was certain to incur her wrath but to leave their encounter that morning without anything further seemed the coward's way out. He simply had to speak with her and make his feelings known.

Seeing her that morning had ignited something within him, a long-buried desire which had never been fulfilled. He had tried his best to forget her, to cast thoughts of her aside, and to imagine his life in a different way. But the sight of her had shown the folly of such action and the foolishness of trying to forget the only woman he had ever truly loved.

"Then I shall call upon her," Louis resolved, "and I shall make her understand.

"Excellent, you can only try, old man," Martin said, reaching over for the plate of tongue and offering further compliments to the piccalilli.

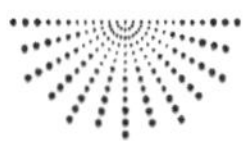

CHAPTER FIVE

"There now, Uncle, your temperature is quite all right," Caroline said, holding up the thermometer for his inspection.

"Are you quite certain, Caroline? I still feel something of the fever," he replied, raising his hand weakly to his forehead.

"You are as strong as an ox. All those years in Africa gave you a constitution unlike anyone else's. You may be a slight man, but you are a strong one and the thermometer does not lie. Even if you yourself may wish to keep me here longer than is my due." Caroline was smiling at her uncle who winked at her.

"I enjoy your company, Caroline, and I wish you had visited me long before now. It is not the same to exchange letters. Sometimes, it is the constancy of companionship that one needs rather than simple words upon a page," he said, as he rang the bell for Perkins.

"And you are always welcome to stay with me in Brimpton Common. I would be delighted to have you there, to live with me even if it is your wish," Caroline said, knowing full well what the response would be.

"Pah, the countryside? My last visit was just awful. Do you remember we were chased by those vicious wild animals?" he cried, throwing his hands up in horror.

"Mr. Pilkington's geese are hardly wild animals and you had strayed into the farmyard when I told you to follow me along the edge of the field. It is no wonder they chased you." Caroline was trying her best to suppress her amusement at the memory.

"Pecked in places I did not know I could be pecked," he replied, tutting at her, as the valet entered the room.

"You rang, sir?" he asked.

"We shall have luncheon here again, Perkins, please. I have no desire to sit at the table; it plays havoc with my foot," Richard said.

The valet nodded. "Very good, sir," he replied, leaving the room to see to the luncheon and leaving Caroline and her uncle alone once again.

"Did you hear any more from the Duke of Norcroft?" Richard asked.

Caroline shook her head. She had told him about the encounter with the Duke and of the pain it had caused her in seeing him once again.

"Not a word and it has been three days since I encountered him," she replied.

"Too cowardly to speak with you, I imagine," Richard said, sitting up awkwardly in his chair.

"I would not wish to speak with him again. You know what he did and how terribly he behaved towards me," she replied.

"Yes, and it sent my favorite niece scampering off into the countryside in search of refuge," he said.

"I like living in the countryside. It was not simply because of Louis that I left London. I am happy with the decision I made," she replied.

"But are you not just a little curious about the whole affair? I remember when it happened you were inconsolable. Your mother told me that for weeks afterward, you moped about the house, lamenting your sorry lot and questioning the man's motives. Now, it seems you have ample opportunity to discover the truth and you shy away from it." Richard raised his eyebrows in question.

He was right, of course, though Caroline had tried her best not to admit it. She did want answers to her questions and she knew that the only way to get them was to speak with the man she had so readily dismissed several days before. In the heat of the moment, she had desired only to see him banished from her side, wishing no further questions or intervention on his part. But in the days which followed, she had grown ever more curious as to discover the truth of what had occurred in the mind of the Duke all those years ago.

"I confess it intrigues me. But only so that I might learn his motives," Caroline replied.

"You were in love with him, were you not? You would have gladly married him, would you have not?" Richard asked.

Caroline nodded. "With all my heart. Which is why it pains me so to now find myself beholden to him once again. My mind says that I should never see him again, but my heart still demands answers as to why it was broken," she replied, as the door opened and Perkins and the maid brought in the luncheon on two large silver trays.

"Pork cutlets, sir," Perkins said, setting the tray down ceremoniously on Richard's knee.

"Splendid, my favorite," he declared, as the silver dome was lifted from the plate.

He dug vigorously into his luncheon, whilst Caroline sat at the table and made an effort to eat hers. She had not felt hungry these past days, her mind dwelling upon the Duke and memories of the past. She found herself despising him and longing to speak with him in equal measures. It was a most peculiar feeling and one which she chastised herself for.

"Then you counsel me to speak with him, Uncle?"

she asked, as he laid down his knife and fork, the plate empty save for the last remnants of gristle and gravy.

"I do, but it must be your choice. To discover where he lives would not be difficult and it would set your mind at ease. You could return to the provincial backwater with answers to the questions which have dogged you these many years past," Richard replied.

"But what of his wife?" Caroline asked.

The question of Lady Victoria Bartlett had plagued her these past few days as equally as her desire for answers from the Duke of Norcroft. In their short encounter, he had made no intimation as to the lady in question nor did there seem to be any evidence as to her part in this sad and sorry state of affairs. Caroline had always assumed that it was she who had been the master architect in the scheme and that surely she had been aware of Caroline's existence long before the marriage was proposed.

"Ah, now, she is something of a mystery though I admit that I do not move in the same social circles. There was some intrigue a few years back, though I was abroad at the time. From what I gather, she lives quietly in the countryside. Though I am not sure if the couple are estranged. The Duke is often seen alone at social gatherings but as for the Duchess, I do not know," Richard replied, now tucking into a bowl of rice pudding.

"It was because of her noble status, that is why he married her and not me," Caroline declared and her uncle shrugged his shoulders.

"Our family had always suffered from its lack of aristocratic credentials. We have money but not status, though we were once titled. The privileges removed when we sided incorrectly in almost every internal conflict this country has known. You possess as much noble blood as Lady Victoria Bartlett, but you suffer from the disgrace of past generations and thus remain a mere commoner in the eyes of many."

"And do you think that the Duke's feelings for me were real? Is it as simple a matter as breeding and title which caused this sadness? I have always wondered as much," she replied.

"Undoubtedly, they were real. I recall seeing the two

of you together and thinking I had seen a perfect match, like two songbirds in the nest. Oh, yes, Caroline my dear, the Duke was in love with you. But he was not allowed to marry below his station. That much is certain," Richard said.

Caroline sighed. Why must such things stand in the way of love? It had seemed so simple when she was young but she knew she had been naïve. Yet she too had fallen in love, deeply in love, a love which remained. Despite her anger at the Duke, she knew too that he may have had little choice in the matter and that she could only seek an explanation from him if her mind was to find some rest in the matter.

"I must speak with him, as much as I do not wish to do so," she said, and her uncle smiled.

"Then you shall have some peace. If you do not speak with him then you are, I am afraid, doomed to be forever tormented by the memory and the questions you hold in your heart. However far you run into the countryside you shall never escape from yourself," he said.

"I did not run away into the countryside, Uncle. But I admit that I do need the answers you speak of.

Otherwise, I shall find myself quite devoid of any hope in the matter and, as you say, I shall never have peace. Do you think you could discover where he lives? This encounter has so preoccupied my mind that I can think of little else," she admitted.

"It will not be difficult to discover the whereabouts of the Duke. I shall ask Perkins to make discreet inquiries. Do not worry, Caroline, we shall find Louis soon enough," Richard said, laying aside his now empty rice pudding bowl.

Caroline nodded, pushing aside her plate, the food still left half-eaten. She had lived so long without answers to the questions of the past that it seemed strange to think that she might soon have them. She had tried her best to forget the Duke and to move on, to leave the past behind, and to focus upon her charitable works and new life in Brimpton Common. But the encounter on Piccadilly had entirely thrown her well-ordered existence up in the air. It had awoken within her new thoughts and feelings and a sense that perhaps there was more to the Duke's behavior in the past than she had realized. Could he be in love with her? Was it merely duty that had prevented their marriage? If so, why had he not had the decency to speak with her?

"I shall take a walk now, Uncle," she said.

"Very good, you do not need to sit with an old man for the rest of the day. Though do you still keep up with pianoforte?" he asked.

Caroline nodded. "You know I do, in my last letter I told you about a wonderful piece of music by Beethoven that I had been practicing," she said.

"Ah, yes, then be so kind as to play for me later on."

"Of course, I will," she replied, and she left him to his book.

She went at once to the morning room, taking quill, ink, and paper before stepping out into the gardens behind the house. They were by no means large, nothing compared to her own garden at the grange, but they were pretty and mature, with the smell of rose and lavender drifting in the breeze. She sat down at a little table on the terrace, pausing a moment to listen to the birds singing above. Apart from her uncle, there was another person whom Caroline trusted to give her advice and she now began to write a long and detailed letter to Anne back in Brimpton Common. She told her of all that had transpired and begged for her advice, though she knew precisely what Anne would say.

She will call him a swine and tell me to have nothing more to do with him, she thought to herself, as she signed the letter and sealed it.

But despite all her misgivings, all her worries and anxieties, Caroline could not rid herself of the tiniest thought that the Duke of Norcroft might not be the swine which she had so long supposed him to be. She had hardly given him the opportunity to explain himself and the manner in which she had dismissed him so readily caused her some distress. She had a charitable and Christian heart, forgiving and willing to listen. She had not allowed herself to listen but now, with her uncle's encouragement, she felt determined to do so.

Next time I write it may be with some more definite answers, she thought to herself, as she handed the letter to the maid for posting.

Now, all that Caroline could do was wait. She would soon discover the whereabouts of the Duke and summon her courage to call upon him. Then, she might receive answers to the questions she so longed for and an explanation of what had occurred all those years ago. That was her hope, at least, and for now, she was content to return to her uncle's side and play the pianoforte for him. Happy in the knowledge that soon she would ask those things so long held in her heart and for which answer thereof might finally give her peace.

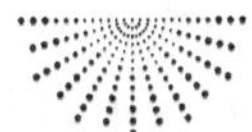

ouis had been restless for a few days. Even though he wanted to, he had made no move to call upon Caroline, embarrassed as to what reception he might receive. Despite Martin's encouragement, which continued over the following days, he could not summon the courage to face Caroline and feel the full force of her wrath. He knew how angry she would be and for him to arrive unannounced would surely make her angrier still.

"I have convinced myself against the idea," he told Martin, as they sat in the drawing room drinking brandy some days after the encounter on Piccadilly.

Martin chuckled, shaking his head. "And now I shall

do what I have done every day these past days and encourage and coax you to change your mind."

It was by now a familiar pattern. Louis would declare himself unable to call upon Caroline, finding any excuse possible to appease himself, before Martin would persuade him of the opposite. By the end of the conversation, Louis would be determined to call upon her immediately; before he acted on it, however, he convinced himself of the folly of such an action.

"But I know she shall turn me down, she will rage at me and with every right to do so," Louis replied.

"A little pain for gain; think what might come of it?" Martin asked, ever the persuasive friend.

Louis sighed; he felt so confused. Since Victoria's death, he had not felt any interest in the company of ladies. She had hurt him so very much and it was only now that he was beginning to recover from his treatment at her hands. But the memory of Caroline had always lingered and this was not the first time that he had thought to contact her. Once, he had got as far as writing her a letter, explaining everything which had happened. But when it came to sending it, he had found himself unwilling, unable, to do so. The letter had been burned and he had told himself to cease his foolish notions and forget her, for there was no hope that Caroline would ever forgive what he had done.

"She is bound to reject me, Martin. I know it," he said, as a knock came at the door.

"A letter for you, Your Grace," Mr. Challoner said, entering the room and casting a wry glance at the half-empty decanter of brandy, which Martin was once again helping himself to.

"A letter? Oh, hand it here, Challoner, thank you," Louis said, not recognizing the handwriting on the envelope.

"Would Mr. Sewell care for further refreshment?" the butler asked.

Louis shook his head. "No, I think Mr. Sewell has had enough refreshment, for now, Challoner, thank you."

Martin blushed. "And who is writing to you, Louis?" he asked, laying aside his half-finished glass of brandy.

"No doubt someone begging for money." Louis rolled his eyes and opened the envelope. As he began to read, his face changed and he smiled, looking up in amazement.

Martin furrowed his brow. "Some interesting news?" he asked.

Louis nodded. "By Jove, it is. Mr. Richard Easton writes, requesting that I meet with Caroline. She is, apparently, keen to speak with me and Richard had his valet search out my address. He says that he hopes it is not an indiscretion on his part but that he knows his niece would appreciate an audience to discuss certain matters. She will call... tomorrow, my goodness. There is little time to prepare," Louis cried, rising from his seat.

"There, you see. It was not for you to judge whether she wished to see you or not. She has made the decision for herself and you are to be the happy recipient of her audience," Martin said, taking up his brandy glass and raising it in a toast.

"Then we must prepare. Challoner, a luncheon, tell the cook to prepare and we must have flowers, yes, cut flowers." Louis rose from his chair with a triumphant look.

"Very good, Your Grace," the butler said, for he was used to his master's fits of enthusiasm.

"I will present her with a bouquet and we shall sit down to a most excellent meal. Wine, Challoner, something of the highest quality from the cellar and send out for some of those delectable cakes from the bakery on The Strand," Louis said, marching to and fro across the room.

"A Charlotte Russe, perhaps?" the butler replied.

"Yes, Challoner, a Charlotte Russe and have the silver polished and the crockery washed. We shall use my great-grandmother's set," Louis said, working himself up into a fever pitch.

"The set which Queen Anne herself dined upon?" the butler asked.

"The very same. Oh, what wonderful news but I must write back," Louis said, a startled look now coming over his face. "I must write and say that Caroline is most welcome and that we shall look forward to seeing her. Quickly, Challoner, bring me quill and ink, I shall write at once."

The butler nodded and went off to bring the necessary implements, leaving Louis and Martin alone.

"It seems you have your wish, my friend," Martin said, finishing his brandy and helping himself to another, now that the butler's all-seeing eye had departed.

"And I must not get it wrong, Martin. I shall have but once chance at explanation and I must do everything I can to make amends," Louis replied.

"You love her enough for that?" Martin asked.

Louis nodded. "I never ceased to love her, Martin. I realize that now." Louis stood wistfully at the window and gazed out across the city.

"Then you must do all you can to salvage what was in the past, my friend," Martin replied.

"I have but one chance. I shall not waste it," Louis replied, the future now appearing somewhat brighter and entirely hopeful, as he looked forward to

Caroline's arrival and the chance that it brought to make good the mistakes of the past.

"Once more if you will, I do love to hear you play," Richard said, as the final notes of the sonata ended and Caroline sat back from the pianoforte.

"I think you find it a most excellent medicine, Uncle," she replied, and her uncle nodded.

"The very best. I wish my own skills were as yours are, my dear girl. Alas, I have practiced too little and been idle for too long. That is why I must listen to you for just as long as you remain here with me and implore you to play as often as you will," he replied.

She sat forward to play again, her fingers moving effortlessly across the keys as she played almost from memory. The pianoforte was one of her great loves and she could so easily be caught up in the music as to be entirely taken into another world. One without care or worry for what lay outside. The music filled the air with the sweetest sound and she glanced up to find her uncle in a similar rapture, his eyes closed, his head back, and a smile on his face.

But a moment later, the sound was interrupted by a commotion in the street outside and a hammering at the door. Richard sat bolt upright and Caroline stopped her playing, listening, as the sound of the maid hurrying to receive their visitor came echoing upstairs. They were not expecting visitors and it seemed their peaceful afternoon was about to be disturbed.

"Whoever can this be?" Richard asked, looking puzzled.

Caroline rose to glance out of the window. But before she could peer out, the door to the sitting room burst open and Anne appeared before them followed by Perkins, who appeared most perturbed by this interruption.

"I came at once," Anne cried.

Caroline began to laugh. "Anne, what a dramatic entrance you have made."

"I had to come at once before it was too late," Anne

replied, throwing her arms around Caroline, who looked ever so surprised.

"Do you know this girl?" Richard asked.

Caroline nodded. "Yes, Uncle. She is my dearest friend and country cousin, Miss Anne Harper. Soon to be the wife of Sir Percy Lindorp," Caroline said.

Anne curtsied to Richard, before turning back to Caroline.

"You have not yet met with the swine, have you?" she asked.

Caroline shook her head. "So, this is what this is all about?" she replied.

Anne nodded. "I could not allow you to face him alone. I have come as a chaperone... if that is to be my task. Your letter spoke of your doubt as to whether or not to see him again. Surely, you cannot be entertaining the idea?" Anne asked, ignoring Perkins and Caroline's uncle.

"Actually... I intend to call upon him tomorrow morning. My uncle has encouraged me to make peace with him and to receive an explanation of what occurred between us all those years ago," Caroline replied.

Anne shook her head. "Then I have come just in time. In my opinion, you are a fool to speak with him, but I know you, Caroline. You are a good and kindly woman with a heart far more charitable than mine. I thought you would do as much, that is why I came at once. I will act as a chaperone and there! will be no dalliance from this man," Anne said.

Caroline smiled. "You are a good and faithful friend, Anne. Now, will you not allow yourself to be introduced properly?" Caroline said, causing Anne to blush.

"A friend of Caroline and clearly one who cares deeply for her welfare is very welcome here," Richard said, struggling to his feet.

"A pleasure to meet you, sir," Anne said. "I am sorry for my abrupt intrusion. But I simply had to see Caroline before..." and she looked at Caroline in some embarrassment.

"Before I met with the swine?" Caroline replied.

Anne nodded. "I do not want you to make a terrible mistake, Caroline," she replied.

Caroline shook her head. "It is only a courtesy call. But you shall accompany me and we shall perhaps have the answers to the questions which I have so long held in my heart," Caroline said.

"And what a coincidence for you to meet him in Piccadilly like that. It must be fate, I suppose," Anne said.

"Perhaps, if it was meant to be." Caroline was wondering what the next day would bring.

"High time for some tea, I think. You must be tired after your journey," Richard said, nodding to Perkins for refreshment.

"Will the lady be staying with us, sir?" he asked.

Richard nodded. "Why, of course, where else would she stay, and besides, I am rather enjoying being surrounded in the company of such charming young ladies. It takes a spirited woman to burst into a man's house like this," he said, winking at Anne, who blushed even further.

The rest of the day was spent in the happiness of

conversation. Anne told Caroline and Richard of the goings-on in Brimpton Common. There was little of note but much of interest, as is the way in the rural backwaters and Caroline told her friend more of her encounter with the Duke and of the feelings he had aroused within her.

"But are you not terribly angry with him?" Anne asked, still referring to the Duke as a swine and a devil.

"I am, but I wish to know more of what transpired between us. I have so many questions. When I saw him first on Piccadilly I was most taken aback and I was angry too. I felt all the frustrations of the past few years erupting, but if my nerves had been calmer then I would have asked for an explanation," Caroline replied.

She had just finished playing the pianoforte for them and had come to sit next to Anne, opposite her uncle.

"But what do you think the explanation can be? He left you for another woman and surely, he is still married to her. What else can he do but reiterate the choice he made and send you on your way?" Anne replied, seemingly still convinced that Caroline was a fool for trying to reignite a spark long since lost without hope.

"He can explain to me why he did it and the reasons behind his silence. That is all I wish for and then we can return to Brimpton Common and have some peace," Caroline replied. "Besides, we have a wedding to plan for."

The arrangements for Anne's wedding to Sir Percy were proceeding like clockwork and they expended much talk that day upon them. But Caroline's thoughts were never far from the Duke, nor the meeting which would take place the next day. Having wished her uncle and Anne a good night, she took to her bed with a nervous heart and found herself unable to sleep or find rest, so nervous was she as to what was to come.

What will he say? Will he give me the explanation I deserve? Her thoughts were like bees, buzzing around her head. Only time would tell what would transpire. She passed a restless night, her mind filled with worry as to what was to come.

"Fortify yourself, my dear, you have quite a day to come," Richard said, as they sat at breakfast the next morning.

In the company of Caroline and now Anne, he appeared to have made a most remarkable recovery. The affliction of his gout was almost entirely ridden. This morning, they sat in the dining room, where any number of tureens and platters were laid out on the sideboard, containing a fine array of foods that had been partly to blame for her uncle's downfall.

"I am not hungry, Uncle," Caroline said, feeling a little nausea as she watched her uncle tuck into the dish of kedgeree with gusto.

"We shall simply make a visit and hear what he has to say. Then we shall leave," Anne said, buttering a slice of bread before adding some jam.

"What am I to wear? What am I to say?" Caroline asked.

Anne laughed, her knife hovering above the bread. "It is not for you to make an impression nor for you to say anything. It is he who owes you an explanation and not the other way around. You look perfectly acceptable as you are, Caroline, and I would hope that he has the words necessary to make you feel at ease. If he does not, then he is not worth your time or effort."

Richard nodded his agreement.

"Then I shall wear what I am wearing and wait for him to speak," Caroline replied.

"We shall leave at eleven o'clock," Anne said, for she had taken it upon herself to take charge of the situation and to see that Caroline was chaperoned whether she wished it or not.

Caroline spent the rest of the morning in something of a nervous frenzy, awaiting the inevitable moment of departure. A hundred thoughts were going around in her head, as she wondered what would transpire between herself and the Duke.

It is merely a conversation, she told herself, as eleven o'clock arrived.

"Good luck, my dear. When you return I am certain you shall have the answers you so desire," Richard said, as she kissed him goodbye.

"I hope so, Uncle," she replied, as she and Anne stepped out of the door.

The carriage was waiting for them and they were soon on their way to the Duke's house, which lay around a mile away on the opposite side of the park. Caroline had not changed her dress, it was plain and simple, and she intended to keep her conversation in a similar vein.

"I shall do my best to hold my tongue," Anne said, as they drew up outside the Duke's house.

"For my sake, Anne, please. You are here as a chaperone, though as my dearest friend too, I know it will be difficult for you to keep from the emotions you feel towards him." Caroline patted Anne's arm.

"I have not even met the man and he angers me," Anne replied, shaking her head.

"The swine," they both said at once, and they fell about laughing, as the carriage pulled up outside the imposing-looking house.

"Come now, there is no turning back," Caroline said, as the carriage driver opened the door.

They waited for a moment before the large door with

its polished brass knocker was slowly opened. It was the butler who greeted them, informing them that his master would be with them soon and they might like to wait in the drawing room. As he showed them through, Caroline noted that the house was lavishly furnished. She could not help but be impressed by the ostentatious wealth displayed around her.

"He must have visited the continent," Anne observed, inspecting a piece of furniture at the side of the room, as Caroline perused the Duke's books.

"Look at this," Caroline said, but before she could point out what she had seen, the door into the room was opened and the Duke of Norcroft appeared before them bearing a large bouquet of flowers.

"Caroline, how wonderful to see you," he said, stepping forward, before looking at Anne in puzzlement.

"Miss Anne Harper, my friend, and chaperone," Caroline said, a little embarrassed by the steely glare which Anne now gave to the Duke.

"A... a pleasure," he said, bowing to her, before coming to present Caroline with the flowers.

"I do not need flowers," she said, declining the Duke's gift.

The flowers drooped in his hands as his face fell. "Ah, well, but you came... that is all that matters... and I am grateful for that," he said, his words stuttering.

"I wished to come. You seemed so eager to make an explanation the other day, that I felt it an imperative that I at least allow you to speak," Caroline said keeping her gaze a little frosty. She had no intention of falling for the Duke's charm. That had been her downfall in the past and she had no wish to see her mistake repeated again.

The Duke nodded, looking somewhat uncertain and embarrassed, just as the clock on the mantelpiece struck twelve. "Ah, luncheon," he said, regaining some of his composure.

"We did not come here for luncheon," Caroline began.

He shook his head. "I assure you there is no ulterior motive on my part, Caroline. Luncheon is all I ask. Will you not join me? There is a veritable feast of delights. Come now," he said as he smiled at her.

Reluctantly, she nodded. Anne rolled her eyes, and the two of them followed the Duke into the dining room where a lavish meal was laid out for them. It seemed that he had gone to an enormous effort to ensure that everything was perfect. The cutlery shone and sparkled in the sunlight coming through the window, the gold-edged crockery and glassware were of the finest quality and a most impressive display of fruit created the centerpiece, with candles lit on every side.

"A most impressive dining room," Caroline said, taking her place.

"I am afraid the table was only laid for two," Louis said, glancing apologetically at Anne, who shrugged her shoulders.

"It is quite all right, I shall wait in here... with the door open," she replied, pointing to the salon which led through from the dining room.

Louis nodded, taking his place opposite Caroline and fixing her with a nervous smile.

"The pate is excellent, or perhaps a little of the boiled ham?" he asked, as the door to the kitchen opened and a maid appeared with yet more dishes in hand.

"A little pate, yes," Caroline said, wishing less to eat than to talk.

"Tell me, what has your life consisted of in these past few years? What delights has the countryside held?" he asked, passing her a plate, as he helped himself to a slice of ham.

"I live quietly enough," she replied, still waiting for him to take the lead in the conversation which truly mattered.

She had not come here to idly discuss her life in the countryside nor to have him show off his wealth and privilege. She had come here for answers, and though the pate was excellent, the setting sublime and the host impeccable in his manners, she was still missing that which she sought.

"You do not bore of life in such a place?" he inquired.

Fixing him with a stern gaze, she shook her head. "The countryside is by no means boring. I have much with which to keep me occupied, thank you. I engage in charitable works, the Church is of great importance to me and I am pleased to say that my life is comfortable when compared to many others. What more should I wish for?"

"But you are enjoying life in the town once again?" he asked.

Caroline was rapidly becoming exasperated by the way he danced around the true issue. Would he ever speak to her directly? She decided to turn the tables and laying down her knife and fork she addressed him more forcefully.

"But what of you, Louis? It's some years since we last saw one another and yet I know nothing of you. How are you enjoying married life? Is it everything *we* hoped for?" she asked, emphasizing her final words in the hope of shaming him into an explanation.

"Well... it was... not as I expected. In fact, it was somewhat fraught. Will you try the salmon? It is excellent with the dill sauce," he said, pointing to the dressed fish on its silver platter.

Caroline could not help but feel a slight sense of satisfaction at this news, knowing that the Duke had chosen badly by rejecting her. It was an uncharitable thought, but one which she felt justified in given her treatment at his hands. Under her gaze, he shifted rather uncomfortably in his chair, making a great pretense of helping himself to further salmon.

"It seems that you got what you deserved," Caroline said, keen now to receive a further explanation of the Duke's behavior.

"Well. Victoria was..." he began, dabbing his mouth with his napkin and almost spilling his glass of wine.

"A formidable opponent and the wrong choice. You passed me over for someone of a higher station. You cared only for your own status and that of your family. My feelings did not come into it.

"Ah... yes... but, Caroline. You must understand that the marriage was far from my choice. I had no desire to marry Victoria, but my family insisted. It was a match of duty and the fulfillment of societal expectations. I had no choice... no choice but to follow their wishes and to marry her," he said, sounding flustered, as though this were not part of his plan for their intimate luncheon.

"And so, you believed it right to treat me in the appalling manner that you did? I may have pitied you for such a thing, even understood the necessities, but you provided no explanation, no hint of pity or of sorrow as to my feelings. I was heartbroken and even more so when you refused to reply to my letters or accept my calling card. I wasted many tears over you, Louis, and for what? Only heartbreak and years of wondering why I was cast aside so readily. You were a coward. You should have stood up to your family, rather than cowering down and marrying a woman of convenient breeding." Caroline lay aside her napkin.

She had heard quite enough now and was ready to leave, but he shook his head, begging her to remain.

"Please, Caroline. You must know that I had every noble intention and I cared deeply for you... I am... I was... in love with you. Truly, I mean it," he said, rising from his place and rushing to her side.

"Then you would surely have fought harder for me. I was ready to marry you, I had convinced myself that we would do so. I had pictured my life with you forever and now I realize how naïve I was to even think that you intended to marry me. All the while you surely had Victoria on your mind and at the first opportunity, you left me for her. If you want to know why I moved to the countryside then look at yourself. You are the reason why. I moved there to escape from you and all the sorrow you brought to me," she said, tears welling up in her eyes.

"Please, Caroline. You must know how much I care for you. I have always cared for you," he began, kneeling at the side of her chair, his eyes wide and imploring.

Caroline glanced through to the salon, catching Anne's eye as she did so. Her friend made a face, shaking her head in disgust, as Caroline turned back to the Duke.

"And you had a fine way of showing it. No letter, no reply to my calling cards. You did not even deign to seek me out and explain. It would have been the simplest of things to do. But you were too cowardly for even that." Caroline shook her head, trying to clear the pain that had haunted her for so many years.

"I was a coward and I was a fool," he said, taking her by the hand.

His touch sent a shiver running through her and she

withdrew her hand with a gasp, as he leaned towards her with a look of utter despondency on his face.

"You were," she said, trying to rise from her chair.

But his hand caught her and he raised his lips towards her cheek, as though he were about to kiss her.

"Goodness me, Louis. How dare you?" she cried, leaping to her feet and slapping his hand away.

He fell backward in a stupor, clutching at the tablecloth, as a glass fell over and Anne came running from the salon.

"Whatever is going on?" she cried, as Louis struggled to his feet.

"Will you not even give me a chance to explain?" he cried, but Caroline had heard enough.

"You have explained enough. I care not for your lies nor for your kiss," she cried.

"A kiss?" Anne said, looking at the Duke in horror.

"But it was not what it seemed. I still love you, Caroline," he said.

Caroline had already swept out into the hallway, followed closely by Anne.

"And you would play me for a fool, as well as your wife? Wickedness indeed, come along, Anne, we are leaving," Caroline cried, snatching up her bonnet from the hat stand and not even waiting for the butler to open the door.

"But it is not like that, she is..." the Duke's voice echoed from the dining room, but Caroline and Anne had already left the house, slamming the door behind them and hurrying down the steps.

"Of all the nerve," Caroline declared, as they hailed the carriage.

"The swine," Anne said, and Caroline could not help but agree.

The Duke had disgraced himself and made himself appear an utter fool. How dare he treat her in such a manner and sully his wedding vows, however difficult he might find married life to be.

"It is quite unbelievable, the nerve of the man," Caroline said, as they rode back to her uncle's house.

She had received the answers to her questions and

knew now that the Duke was nothing but the foppish rake she had suspected him to be. A man without a backbone. One who cared only for himself and his needs in the moment. Well, she had no intention of being part of it. As they arrived home, she knew she would be happy never to see the Duke again.

"Good riddance to him," Anne said.

Caroline nodded. "Yes, he has proved himself to be everything I suspected. Good riddance to him, indeed."

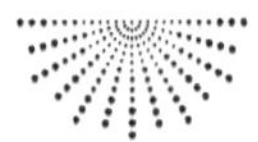

CHAPTER SEVEN

*L*ouis sat dejectedly at the table, surrounded by the detritus of the lavish luncheon. He had refused Mr. Challoner's request to clear the table and was toying with a bowl of Charlotte Russe when a knocking came at the door.

"Mr. Sewell is here to see you, sir," the butler said, "shall I show him into the drawing room?" Challoner cast his eye across the wine-soaked table cloth and half-finished dishes.

"Yes," Louis replied, rising from his place, his shoulders sagging.

When he entered the drawing room, Louis found

Martin helping himself to brandy. His friend looked up with an eager expression on his face, though his mood was shortly cowed by the look which Louis gave him in return.

"Am I to infer that the interview with Caroline did not go according to plan?" he asked.

Louis nodded. "You might say that. It was a disaster and I was a fool." Louis slumped into the chair opposite.

Martin poured him a large brandy, pushing it under his nose in an attempt to revive him.

"Did she spurn you?" he asked.

Louis nodded. "More than that. I behaved in a most dishonorable manner."

"You did not...?" Martin began.

"The fool I am," Louis said, shaking his head.

"Really, Louis. What stupidity. Come now, tell me everything," he said.

Louis recounted the events of the luncheon and how he had tried his best to explain his side of the story.

But the attempted kiss had been his downfall and he knew it. Such foolishness was hardly the order for success. It was no wonder that Caroline had so readily dismissed him and left with the declaration of never seeing him again. He had tried to explain to her that his marriage to Victoria was far from happy and that it was taken up out of a sense of duty, rather than desire. But Caroline had not wanted to listen and now it seemed there was little hope that she ever would.

"And so, she left the house with her chaperone and that was that," Louis said, sighing once more.

"And you think there is no hope of salvaging the situation and making her see things differently?" Martin asked, ponderously swirling the brandy in his glass.

"I think that she has made her position very clear. She told me I was betraying not only her but my wife too," he replied.

"But your wife is dead, Louis. You are no longer married in the sight of state or God. Of that, we can all agree. Caroline does know this, does she not?" Martin raised his eyebrows.

"I was not able to explain it to her before she left. The situation was... somewhat... delicate," Louis replied, taking a sip of brandy.

"Then there is still hope, surely? She does not know the full truth and if she did then she would see your attempt to kiss her as a reconciliation rather than a scandal. Of that, I am certain." Martin folded his arms and nodded, showing that he was convinced the matter could be resolved.

"But it is in itself a scandal to reveal the tragic circumstances of Victoria's death. To do so would reopen old wounds and lead to my ruin if it were discovered," Louis replied.

"Then what is it you want, Louis? You cannot both pretend to still be married and yet also desire to court Caroline once more. Your feelings betray you, my friend. The scandal would not be so great as you think. It is Victoria who disgraced herself and not you. She is dead, the matter is settled and you are free to marry whomsoever you wish," Martin declared, raising his brandy glass in a toast.

"But what difference would it make? She is obviously not willing to listen to me. I should never have courted her company again." He blew out as if trying to push the thing from his mind. "How I wish I had not walked along Piccadilly that day. That way I would never have met her again. I hope she returns to the country very soon and that I never have to see her again." Louis banged his fist down on the arm of the chair.

"I do not believe that you mean that, Louis. I think you want to see her again and explain the mess you got yourself into... In fact, you must make her see, for it sounds to me that your dalliance around the matter led to your downfall. The luncheon, the flowers, the polite conversation, all of it meant nothing. She needs to simply know that Victoria is dead, that you regretted the marriage into which you were forced, that you are remorseful, and that you are still in love with her. It is that simple," Martin said, helping himself to another glass of brandy from the now empty decanter.

When expressed in such terms the matter appeared utterly simple. Caroline did need to know the facts as they stood and know the truth about Victoria. But Louis wondered if he had the strength to face her again and make his desires known. The more he thought of her the more he knew he was still in love and that his love for her had never dwindled. It had pained him deeply to leave her as he did, but at the time he thought it was best for both of them. Seeing her when he could not marry her was too much to bear.

He still remembered the woeful moment when his father forbade him from marriage to a 'commoner,' and the tears he shed on Caroline's behalf. He had been young and naïve, believing the best thing for both of them was a clean break. But try as he might, the years had not lessened the feelings in his heart and the love he felt for Caroline. In fact, they were now even stronger. He wished beyond hope that she might believe the sincerity of his words if they were to meet again. The last thing he wanted was for her to disappear back into the countryside, all he wanted was to have her at his side.

"I do not mean it, Martin. Far from it in fact. But what am I to do?" Louis asked, putting his head in his hands.

"It is very simple, how many times must I say it, Louis? You must tell her everything and make her understand what has transpired in all this time that has passed. Water under the bridge, the passage of time, that is what has occurred and she must surely come to see that," Martin said.

"But she may still spurn me." he moaned.

Martin shook his head in exasperation. "Perhaps, but you will be exonerated from your guilt. She will have the facts before her and if she still chooses to reject you then so be it. That is for her to decide and for you to live with. But you cannot possibly allow yourself to leave things as they are now. That offers no peace for either of you," Martin declared.

"Perhaps we could at least be friends and recover something of the spark between us," Louis said, his mind filling with a fresh sense of hope.

"That is the spirit, now, are there any leftovers from lunch? I am famished." Martin rose from his chair and rang the bell.

Mr. Challoner appeared a moment later and Martin asked for him to bring a tray of leftovers so that they might dine and talk at the same time. Louis did not feel like eating, but his friend tucked in ravenously and continued to persuade him as to the merits of speaking with Caroline again.

"I shall be dreadfully nervous," Louis said.

Martin laughed. "Of course, you will be, but you have no need to be. You are simply telling the truth and no man should be nervous of the truth. It is far better than to live a lie. Many men fall by such a sword. After all, you have not so much lied to Caroline, but you have made her think the situation to be very different from the facts. A foolish thing to allow and now you have the chance to rectify it and you must do so."

"And upon what pretense am I to call upon her?" Louis asked, thinking that the arrangement of an interview would be far easier said than done.

"You simply call at the house and ask to see her. Tell the maid, or the valet, or whoever, that you have an important piece of information for her. No woman could surely resist such an allure. She will see you, she will be too intrigued not to," Martin replied, slathering a piece of bread with pate and topping it with a slice of tongue.

"Then I will call upon her, I have nothing to lose," Louis replied, trying to sound far more confident than he felt.

"Nothing at all, my friend," Martin replied. "Now, shall we have another drink?"

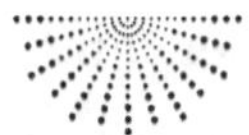

CHAPTER EIGHT

Caroline had taken to her bed upon arriving back at her uncle's house. She had been so shocked by her treatment at the hands of the Duke and the scandalous way in which he had behaved, that she felt quite out of sorts. She did not even speak with Richard but bid Anne a good afternoon and shut herself away in her chambers. Her head was aching and her whole body was wracked with a terrible weakness. Brought on, no doubt, by the emotional turmoil she had ensured at Louis' hands.

She felt so confused by his actions and wondered what on earth he could have been thinking. It was one thing to break off an engagement in favor of another woman but to be so flagrant as to seek adultery was another thing entirely. It shocked her to imagine Louis in such terms and the scandal which could so easily have been caused was quite beyond her. The night before she had hardly slept and it seemed as if her body wished to catch up. Soon, she fell into a deep slumber, and she slept for much of the afternoon, rising only to take a light supper by the window before taking to her bed once more.

In the morning, things appeared clearer, she was no longer enveloped in the emotional turmoil and anger with which she had returned home. Instead, she could only pity the Duke for the recklessness of what he had done. Now, she saw in him a contemptible figure, one to be forgotten. She would not allow these happenings to send her into the turmoil she had experienced in her youth. The Duke was of no consequence to her and she fully intended to forget him.

However, her heart was tricky. It mourned her lost love and it was a decision easier made than done. As she made her way down to breakfast that morning, she still found her mind to be preoccupied with thoughts of the Duke and the explanation he had given her. It was hardly an adequate one, though she could still find some pity for the predicament of his situation. She had known his father to be a hard man. One who placed duty over all else. It was hardly surprising that he demanded his son's complete obedience and made no accommodation for love or the feelings of the heart. Still, she could not forgive a man so willing to discard his marriage vows for the sake of a stolen kiss. Thinking back on the events of yesterday and the potential scandal it might cause, brought a wave of anger that she had never felt before.

"Ah, Caroline, my dear," Richard said, as she entered the dining room.

"Are you fully rested?" Anne asked.

Caroline nodded.

"You had a terrible shock. Anne told me all about it last night. I cannot believe that a married man, a man of such standing and one who should command respect, should think it to be his right to treat you in such a manner... and to expect your reciprocation. You preserved your honor, Caroline, and for that, you must be commended," Richard said.

Caroline felt as if a knife was twisted in her gut. Why had he treated her so? "He behaved atrociously. I am only glad that I did not marry him. If that is how he respects the wife he chose over me then however would he have treated me if we had been married?"

"He was forced to choose her, I understand?" Richard said, helping himself from a dish of devilled kidneys.

"He was... but he could have chosen to reject his father's instructions and the two of us could have been happy. What is more, he could have found it in him to offer me an explanation of why he behaved in such a manner, rather than keeping silent for so long." Caroline reined down her anger, but like a startled horse, it wished to bolt.

"You have seen his true colors and have come to realize that the Duke of Norcroft is far from the man he should be. At least you did not succumb to his advances. I was worried that perhaps his charm might overwhelm you and that you would find yourself at his mercies," Richard said.

"I am a stronger woman than that, Uncle. You know that," Caroline replied.

She was fiercely independent and had no intention

of allowing the Duke of Norcroft, or any man for that matter, to get the better of her. In affairs of the heart, Louis had taught her one thing and that was to be cautious. Her caution had paid off and she was not about to fall for his charms or empty words, not after she had seen him for who he truly was.

"And what now? I suppose you will tell me that the two of you intend to return to Brimpton Common? Anne has told me all about her wedding plans and even issued me with an invitation. But I shall be sad to see the two of you leave. I am growing rather accustomed to your company. We played a splendid game of cards last night, did we not, Anne?" Richard said as Anne joined them at the table.

"We did. I do like it here, though I know you prefer the peace of the countryside, Caroline," Anne replied.

"We have your wedding to prepare for. But I must admit, apart from my dalliances with the Duke, I have enjoyed my time with you, Uncle. I will not stay away for as long next time, I promise. But if you are invited to Anne's wedding then you will *have* to visit us in our rural backwater and stay with me at the grange. There is always a bedroom made up for you and the village will always make you very welcome," Caroline said.

"Even those geese?" Richard said, winking at them both.

"Even the geese," Caroline replied.

"Splendid, then perhaps I am somewhat more attracted to the idea of life in the countryside, especially if I am looked after as well as I have been these past few weeks."

"You have always been well looked after, Uncle, but I admit that I have enjoyed being here, as has Anne. I will not keep my distance from London in quite the same manner as before. But I could never live here again," she said.

"I must admit, there are times when I long to be elsewhere. Perhaps still on my adventures abroad, but I love the city and could not imagine living anywhere else," Richard said.

"Then we must agree to disagree on that particular matter," she replied.

The three of them passed a pleasant breakfast and for a few moments, Caroline found herself able to forget her ordeal at the hands of the Duke. It would, in time, become a simple memory and one to drift away into the mists of time. It had to be thus if she were to truly move on and put her feelings aside. She had come so close to disaster once again at the hands of a man she had once loved so passionately and who it seemed could do nothing but betray her.

She could not believe the pity she had felt for him, nor the sympathy in her heart for his sad marital situation. He had made his choice and now he must live with it. Just as she was forced to live with her own mixed and conflicting feelings. Her first love would surely be her last and though unrequited and foolish, she still felt those first pangs of love in her heart, a fire still smoldering for the Duke. It was a ridiculous thing, but to fall out of love with someone was far harder than falling in love with them and the tangled web of their emotions made her realize just how much she once had hoped upon him, depended upon him and needed him.

Well, not anymore. I am determined of that, she thought to herself, as she and Anne made their way out into the garden.

"What a beautiful day, perhaps we should take

advantage of our days in town and do something delightful," Anne said, smiling at Caroline.

"What might you suggest? A walk in the park perhaps or some shopping on Piccadilly? You would love Mr. Hatchard's bookshop," Caroline replied.

"Yes, the bookshop. I can buy a present for Percy, he loves reading and it would make an excellent memento of my time in town," Anne replied.

"We shall take our morning cup of tea and then depart," Caroline said, as they settled down on the terrace, gazing out across the pretty garden beyond, just as Richard came hurrying outside.

"Caroline, he is here," he cried.

Caroline looked up in astonishment. "Who is here?" she asked.

Richard looked nervously over his shoulder.

"The Duke of Norcroft. Perkins has just announced him, what are we to do?" he said, shaking his head and appearing all of a dither.

"The swine," Anne cried, "how dare he come here

after what he has done. You cannot possibly receive him, Caroline."

"I shall tell Perkins to send him away. He has no right to interfere in such a manner. To call upon you when he has behaved in such a way is simply wicked." Richard nodded his agreement.

For a moment, Caroline was stunned into silence. She could see no reason why the Duke should be calling upon her unless of course, it was to offer an explanation for his actions. But it seemed his actions had been clear and what further reason should there be for causing her such distress?

"I... but..." she began.

Anne rose from her seat. "I shall tell him myself," she said.

Caroline raised her hand. "No... I... I shall hear what he has to say. He has clearly come either to beg or to explain. If he is to beg then I shall send him away but if he is to explain then I shall listen," she replied.

"But you cannot possibly wish to hear him." Richard was shaking his head.

"I do want to hear him and that shall be the end of it.

I shall tell him never to trouble me again and to ensure that this is the end of our acquaintance. I wish nothing more to do with him, except to hear what he has to say and be done with it," Caroline replied.

Richard sighed and Anne scowled, but Caroline was determined and taking a deep breath, she made her way inside. There, she found Perkins hovering in the drawing room and she nodded to him, instructing him to show the Duke upstairs to the sitting room.

"Very good, ma'am," Perkins replied, and she listened at the door as the valet gave her instructions to the Duke.

Hold your nerve, Caroline, she told herself, as she waited a few moments, before making her way upstairs.

She paused for a moment outside of the sitting room, listening to the Duke pacing up and down. She smiled to hear the nervous tapping of his feet, knowing that she, not he, was in control of the situation. She drew herself up to her full height, ready to face whatever words he had to give her and opened the door.

The Duke looked nervous as she entered and bowed low, his hands were shaking. She made no remark, but settled herself down in a chair and made no invitation for him to do the same. He looked like a naughty child, waiting for his mother's wrath, and he began to gabble indistinctly before she raised her hand.

"Enough," she said.

He let out a deep sigh and slumped into her uncle's favorite armchair.

But at that moment, the door burst open and Richard appeared before them.

"I am sorry, Caroline, but I simply could not bear to allow you to face this man alone. You, Your Grace, are a disgrace. You have toyed with my niece's affections and behaved in a most scandalous and unbecoming manner. How dare you come here and expect an audience at will, it is quite unheard of," Richard cried.

Louis seemed to shrink even further.

"But I ..." the Duke began.

"An adulterer. That is what you are, nothing but an adulterer," Richard cried, banging his hand down on the nearest piece of furniture.

Caroline watched the Duke's reactions. He seemed pained, perplexed even at the insults which her uncle now levied at him. What would his reply be? She wanted him to take the lead and explain himself, for she had no intention of making things easy for him. Quite the opposite in fact.

"Sir, I come here in all sincerity and with an openness of heart to offer my apologies and to seek forgiveness," Louis began.

"A forgiveness you could have sought without subjecting my niece to your lascivious designs," Richard replied, shaking his head and tutting.

"You call me an adulterer, but I think that you have been misinformed or rather have not been privy to the truth," Louis said.

At these words, Caroline looked at him strangely. What other word could there be for a man who forgot the vows of his wedding day and chose instead to seek another woman's affections? Was the Duke married or was he not?

"Misinformed?" Richard said, his voice now lower and sounding puzzled.

"I did marry Lady Victoria Bartlett, as I explained to Caroline. It was a mistake and I should have been stronger in my objections. But my father and mother were insistent and I had little choice but to obey. But Victoria was not the woman I was led to believe. The morality of a person is not dependent upon the grace imparted by a title, far from it in fact. Victoria was a philanderer, a woman who courted men from London to Bath and who was unafraid to make a show of it," the Duke said, the emotion rising in his voice.

"What do you mean, 'was' a woman?" Richard asked.

"If you will let me explain, sir, I shall tell you. I was faithful to my marriage vows and prepared to look the other way but upon my return from the continent on business I discovered she was mixed up with a treacherous scoundrel named Count Giovanni Battisto, an Italian of ill repute and one whom she betrayed with another man. Well, he did not take kindly to this and Victoria was... murdered," he said, shaking his head with sorrow.

Caroline let out a cry, for it seemed too incredible for words and Richard recoiled in shock.

"Murdered? But I thought..." he began, and the Duke shook his head.

"Imagine the scandal, if all of London had discovered it. It was better to keep the whole thing a secret, than risk the reputation of myself and the family. Since her death, I have put it about that Victoria is ailing and spends her time locked away from the world at my country estate. It is far easier that way. I assure you, however foolish my actions of yesterday, they were not adulterous. Foolish yes, but adulterous, no," the Duke said.

"But such a thing is unthinkable. How could she have been killed and no one knows?" Richard said, shaking his head in disbelief.

"Who knows what secrets are hidden within plain sight in this city, sir?" the Duke replied.

"He is telling the truth," Caroline said, her voice sounding weak and distant.

This revelation had turned everything upside down. She was astonished to think that for all these years the Duke had lived in the secrecy of his wife's scandal. It was no scandal of his but how terrible that he should have been subjected to such a thing. Her sympathies were aroused but she could not help but think he had still been a heartless fool to spurn her as he had done.

"What happened between Victoria and me, does not excuse my behavior. I was a young, naïve, and foolish man. My father told me I must never contact you, my mother told me it would best for you if I didn't. I believed my mother. I believed the pain of seeing me again would cause you the same pain I felt. I believed I was doing the right thing by making a clean break. Oh, what a foolish child I was! So easily led. The pain I felt was beyond understanding and I now know that you felt the same. I cannot take that back... I can only apologize once again. My actions of yesterday were that of a desperate man who longed to make amends to the woman he... was a fool to lose all those years ago."

Caroline did not know what to say or what to think. But his voice was filled with such sincerity that she felt inclined to think well of him. He was being truthful, completely truthful, and exposing himself to the potential of scandal and disgrace. And for what? Did he love her? Were those the words he was holding back and what were her own feelings towards him now? She felt a sense of tenderness towards him, he no longer seemed the cruel and heartless man she had once declared him as, nor the swine whom Anne had judged him to be. He was the victim of foolishness, weakness, certainly. He was misled by his parents and subjected to the machinations of a cruel and heartless woman. But she no longer believed that his unhappiness was what he deserved; instead, she could see beyond the past to the man now stood meekly before her, willing to tell the truth.

"You truly believe that?" she asked.

He nodded. "I do, but I shall willingly take my leave of you now. I came here for no other reason but to tell the truth and I have done so to the best of my ability. You know everything now, Caroline, the whole truth. It is not something I am proud of, but I hope that you will understand why I did what I did and why I behaved so irrationally yesterday. I only wanted to make you understand, I still have feelings for you. Feelings long buried but which resurfaced the moment I laid eyes upon you on Piccadilly. Surely, it was fate."

Caroline felt a surge of warmth inside, something was awakening, something she couldn't fully comprehend right now. "I thank you for your honesty," she replied.

"Then I shall take my leave of you. I have wasted enough of your time, Caroline. Mr. Easton, may I apologize to you for bursting in like this? I wish you a swift recovery from your ailments and a good day," the Duke said, preparing to take his leave.

"No, Louis, will you stay a moment?" she said, looking up at him and smiling.

His expression changed, a look of hope and longing appearing in his eyes.

"Why, yes," he said, smiling at her, as she motioned him to sit again.

"Would you excuse us, Uncle?" Caroline said.

Richard nodded. "I shall re-join Anne in the garden," he said, still eyeing the Duke with some suspicion.

"I assure you, sir, my intentions are honorable," the Duke said, bowing to Richard, as he left the room.

Caroline motioned again for him to take a seat, fixing him with what she hoped was a sympathetic look. Her feelings towards him had entirely changed. The revelation of his sad treatment at the hands of his wife and the disaster that had been their marriage now seeming to be a cause for sympathy rather than a delight in revenge. It seemed he had been entirely unlucky in love. A disastrous marriage forced upon him by his cruel and overbearing parents. How different things might have been if only he had been bolder in his youth.

"But I still do not understand why you did not try to contact me sooner upon the death of your wife. Did you think I would be scandalized? Quite the opposite, I would have understood. I may even have been able to help you," she said, shaking her head.

"Dearest Caroline, I thought about it. I even wrote you a letter, but the fool in me tore it up before I could post it. I had heard of your move to the country and the fact that you rarely visited town. I thought that you had cut your ties once and for all. You had every right to do so and I had no right to interfere in your life once more. I was embarrassed too. For a man of my standing to be treated in such a way by his wife is unheard of. I would be a laughing stock," he replied.

"For what reason? It is she who behaved so appallingly towards you. That is no fault of yours," Caroline replied,

"And yet I feel it is," the Duke said, sighing and looking down at his feet.

"You have nothing to be ashamed of," she repeated, reaching out and taking his hand.

A sudden wave of tenderness had run through her. No longer did she see the cruel-hearted man her mind's eye had so conjured over the years. Instead, she saw a man who had entirely lost his way. A man clinging to a lie which would forever hold him back, unless the truth was finally told.

"I thought perhaps that you had found happiness with another. As would be your right. I pictured you and hoped that you were enjoying all the good things which I had denied you through my foolishness," the Duke said.

Caroline laughed. "I had no desire for such things, not after the way in which we parted company. I was a broken woman, my heart shattered into a thousand pieces, never to be repaired. I could not imagine life with anyone else but you and so I threw myself into charitable works and made myself a spinster for the sake of my own well-being. It was not my choice but it was the right thing to do. I could not have lived had

I not done so. I pushed your memory far down into my soul and kept it there, allowing myself only fleeting remembrances and even those caused me pain. When I saw you on Piccadilly the other day it aroused such a feeling in me as to be overwhelming," she said, surprised to find a tear welling up in her eye.

"I had the same feelings. I too had tried my best to leave the past behind. You do not know what guilt I felt at what I had done. I was a fool and I hurt you. For that, I can only ask forgiveness," he replied.

"You should have told me the whole story from the beginning, I would have understood," she said.

Once again he sighed.

She watched, as he rose from his chair and went to the window, their hands parting as he stood with his back to her.

"But will the world out there understand, Caroline? I do not think so," he said, turning back to her and shaking his head.

"And what does the world matter? It is... you and I who matter. I would have understood, even if I was angry with you at first. But you have my forgiveness, of that I assure you. I understand that your parents forced you into that loveless marriage and that you felt duty-bound to honor it. There was nothing you could have done and I admire you for your fidelity, even in the face of your wife's philandering," Caroline said.

At these words of forgiveness, the Duke's whole countenance changed and it seemed as though a great weight had been lifted from his shoulder. He smiled at her and came to kneel before her, taking her hand in his and gazing up at her with such a look of adoration that it quite took her breath away.

"I do wish that I could erase the past, Caroline, and begin again. Do you remember that first moment when we met? And how we danced together the whole night? It was the most perfect night of my life and I have treasured its memory ever since. How I long to return to such simple times and know again the innocence of that youth we shared. Alas, it has been tainted by what has come since and my experiences have left such a sour taste. But to hear you pronounce those words of forgiveness has truly made my heart soar."

"You have my forgiveness and I too long for that night. It was the happiest night of my life too, though I admit I was naïve and taken up by all that it contained. Perhaps we were not ready for... the feelings it caused within us," she replied.

He nodded, still clutching her hand. "How I wish to begin again... if only you would let me."

"Perhaps together we could lay the past to rest and begin again," she said.

The Duke's eyes grew wide and a broad smile broke across his face.

"Your forgiveness means the world to me and you must know that I would never be such a fool again," he said.

"It must have been a lonely life, even when Victoria was alive. You have lived your own exile in a way, just as I have. I sought refuge in the countryside in the hope that it would lay my feelings to rest. But I must admit that there were times when I could have screamed at the closeness of Brimpton Common and rushed back to London in the hope of escaping once more. It is impossible to flee from one's own self, however hard one tries," she said.

"We have both been prisoners of the past and how sorry I am that our prison could not have been together," he said.

"I often thought of you," she admitted, laughing and shaking her head.

"As did I of you, every day in fact," he said.

"I would chastise myself for it and tell myself I was a fool even to contemplate you. But your vision would be there and I would wonder what you were doing and if you were happy. Now I know that you were not," she said.

"I was miserable. Victoria and I had nothing in common but an aristocratic title. We cared not for the same pleasures and almost as soon as we were married, we began to drift apart. I spent more and more time in town, drinking with my friend, Martin, and wiling away the hours at my club. And all the while she was... well, you know what she was doing," the Duke said, blushing a little.

"She sounds the most frightful of women," Caroline said.

"Frightful is the word, though we should not speak ill

of the dead. She had her problems, many problems in fact, but I should not think ill of her for that, now," he replied.

Caroline smiled at him. She had forgotten what a good man he was. It was one of the many reasons why his behavior all those years ago had been so shocking. He *was* a good man, a kind and charitable man, whose heart had always been concerned with others. In the years of their youth, she had seen his good works and heard his hopes for the future. But it seemed that his treatment at the hands of his wife had almost broken him and he was no longer the man he once had been. Now, he was a shadow of his former self.

"I can still see you as you once were," she said, causing him to blush.

"A rash and overbearing youth?" he asked, laughing as he spoke.

"No, a kind man with a heart of gold, the man I fell in love with all those years ago. The glimmer is still there, I can see it in you and I would like to fan it into a flame," she said, reaching out to take his other hand in hers.

"You mean ...?" he began.

She nodded. "I always wondered whether there might be a chance to rekindle what we once had. I tried so hard to forget it, but the thought was always there. Perhaps fate has now brought us together for a reason. When we met outside Mr. Hatchard's bookshop I thought that I never wished to see you again, yet my heart told me differently. At first, it was only answers which I craved, answers you have now given me. But now, it is something else, something we have both lost but now found," she said.

Their hands were joined together, and they gazed into one another's eyes. To Caroline, it felt just like that moment all those years ago, when she had gazed into that same pair of eyes and known that she was looking at the only man she could ever love. On that occasion, he had leaned forward and kissed her, whispering sweet nothings in her ear and promising her that they would be together forever.

Now, the years had passed and much had transpired, but it was the same look of love she now beheld and the same feelings which arose in her heart. She loved him and she knew that he loved her too. The years did not matter, the things they had endured did not matter, the past did not matter, only the moment, as he leaned forward once again and kissed her.

"May we make up for the time we have lost?" he whispered.

"There is much time ahead, it is not too late to do so," she replied, and he kissed her once again.

"I never stopped loving you but now I think I love you even more," he whispered.

She smiled at him, rising to her feet and taking him by the hand. She led him to the pianoforte and sat down, as he put his arms around her shoulders.

"Do you remember this?" she asked, and she began to play a sonata from memory, the same one they had danced to on the very first evening they had been together.

"How could I forget it? This was the music with which I fell in love," he said, as she continued to play and the past seemed to heal itself, the future lying ahead.

Caroline could not have felt happier; in that moment all the troubles of the past seemed to melt away. As the music echoed through the air, she knew her own burden was lifted. No longer was she bound by the past but excited by the future. The years gone by seemed as nothing and it was as though she and Louis had taken up precisely from the moment they had parted.

"May this be the start of something wonderful," she said, and he shook his head.

"Only the continuation of what was wonderful, to begin with," he replied, leaning down and kissing her again.

CHAPTER TEN

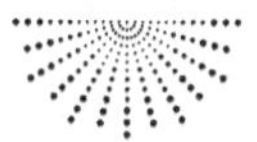

It was two months later and the day of Anne's wedding to Sir Percy Lindorp. Much had transpired since that fateful afternoon in the sitting room of Caroline's uncle and she was looking forward immensely to spending this special day celebrating with her friend.

"Come now, Uncle. We shall be late if you do not hurry," she called up the stairs from the hallway, as her uncle appeared on the landing.

"How I wish I had brought Perkins with me. I am not used to making my own arrangements in the dressing room. Tell Louis to come and help me, I have already broken two collar studs. Susan is an excellent maid, but she seems to have rather over starched my collar. I fear it is as sharp as a guillotine," Richard called back.

Caroline stifled her laugh behind her hand. "Louis, would you go and help my uncle? He is having trouble with his collar," she called out, as her husband appeared from the dining room.

He was already dressed in his wedding finery, with a blue frock coat and breeches, a pristine white tunic shirt and a cravat in yellow and red polka dots. He grinned at Caroline, leaning in to kiss her, as he made his way up the stairs.

"Fear not, sir, help is on its way," he called out, as Challoner appeared behind him.

"Would you like me to attend to this, Your Grace?" the butler asked.

"No, no, let me sort it," Louis said. "You have other things to attend to."

Challoner raised his eyebrows at Caroline and left.

Caroline could not contain the smile that spread across her face. The two of them had been married in a simple ceremony only a week after their reconciliation. It had, as each of them pointed out, been like taking up from precisely where they left off and neither felt the need for a lavish ceremony or a celebration filled with the great and the good. The marriage had taken place quietly and there was not a hint of scandal for the name of Victoria was not mentioned, except to the clergyman who assured them of his discretion. The only guests had been Richard, Anne, and Martin Sewell, who had acted as witnesses and accompanied the happy couple for a lavish meal at Rules Restaurant. From there, they had returned to Brimpton Common and were now living happily together at the grange.

"That is the third one," Caroline heard Richard cry out, and she hurried upstairs, to find Louis and Richard engaged in a bizarre looking dance as they tried to fix the collar onto the shirt.

"He will not stand still," Louis said.

Caroline fell about laughing, as Susan, the maid, appeared from one of the bedrooms.

"What a spectacle, Susan. You would think His

Grace and my uncle had never put on a collar between them before," Caroline said.

"Please, ma'am, I think Mr. Easton has the collar on backward," Susan said, raising her eyebrows.

"Backward?" Richard cried, "of course it is not backward, Susan. What are you talking about?"

"Ah…" Louis said, and he removed the collar and turned it upside down.

"Backward," Caroline said, shaking her head, as she and Susan exchanged womanly glances.

With her uncle now properly attired the three of them made their way downstairs. It was a beautiful summer's day, the perfect day for a wedding and Samuel Timpson, with the horse and carriage, had just arrived to collect them. It was only a short distance to the church, but they wished to arrive with all the ceremony which such an occasion demands. Caroline was to act as a bridesmaid, but Anne had an army of younger sisters and cousins to assist her in her preparations and she had told her closest friend to simply be at the church on time.

It was close to eleven o'clock and they pulled up

outside Saint Bartholomew's, just as Anne herself was arriving with her entourage in an open-topped carriage bedecked with bunting. She looked so pretty, in a peach wedding dress, with a bouquet of red roses and a long trailing veil. She waved to Caroline, who hurried over to help her down and embraced her.

"You look so beautiful, Anne. You really do," Caroline exclaimed, as Louis and Richard came up behind her.

"Ah, here is the blushing bride-to-be. You look wonderful, my dear. Sir Percy is a lucky man. If I had been but a few years younger, then he would not have stood a chance," Richard said.

Caroline tutted. "Really, Richard," she said, but Anne just laughed, as her father climbed down from the carriage and took her arm.

"Now, all we need is Mr. Hickson. I trust the groom has arrived," he said, just as the rector emerged from the church in his billowing white surplice.

"Ah, Lord Brimpton, dear Anne, Sir Percy is here and waiting. We can begin immediately," he said.

Lord Brimpton nodded.

"Certainly, sir, my nerves cannot take the impending excitement any longer," he said, smiling around at them.

Louis and Richard made their way into the church. Caroline was left with Anne and Lord Brimpton at the door.

"You really do look ever so beautiful, Anne. I am so happy for you," Caroline said, kissing her on the cheek.

"It is the happiest day of my life. Just as your own wedding day was for you," Anne replied.

Caroline nodded. "It seems an age ago, yet it is only a few weeks. I have settled into married life so quickly and I know you will too. Sir Percy is such a wonderfully kind man, he really is," Caroline said, as Mr. Hickson returned from the front of the church.

"The groom is ready, Anne, and the organist awaits my signal. Are you ready?" he asked.

Anne nodded. "I think so," she replied.

"Then let us begin," the rector said, signaling to the

organist who struck up the chords of the hymn and they made their way into the church.

It was packed full of people, for the marriage of Lord Brimpton's eldest daughter was an important event for the whole village. Heads turned and necks were craned as everyone tried to get a look at the bride, as she made her way solemnly down the aisle. Caroline caught Louis's eye, blushing a little as he smiled at her. She knew he had eyes only for her and already the memories of that happiest day when they had wed were flooding back.

As they arrived at the front of the church, Sir Percy turned to look at his bride. He was a handsome man, with blond tousled hair and bright blue eyes. Now, he smiled at them, as Anne slipped her arm from her father's and into his, smiling and whispering a greeting to him. Caroline and Lord Brimpton stepped back, and she made her way to the pew where Louis and Richard waited. The hymn was in its midst and she slipped her arm into Louis' and leaned her head on his shoulder.

"What a perfect day," she whispered to him.

"Just like our own," he replied, as the last of the organ notes resounded through the church.

"Dearly beloved, we are gathered together here in the sight of God, and in the face of this Congregation, to join together this man and this woman in Holy Matrimony..." Mr. Hickson began, as the marriage service commenced.

Caroline watched, as her friend made the same vows she had made just a few weeks before. They promised to love and cherish one another in sickness and in health, for richer and poorer, and until death did them part. The look on Anne's face spoke of the same happiness she had felt when she and Louis had pronounced their vows. A happiness she still felt even now.

"And now the kiss," Caroline whispered, leaning up to Louis, who turned and smiled at her.

"I pronounce that they be husband and wife together. In the Name of the Father, and of the Son, and of the Holy Ghost. Amen," Mr. Hickson concluded, holding out his hands, as the congregation applauded.

Caroline watched, as Sir Percy took his bride in his

arms and the two shared a kiss, one which she and Louis now imitated. It was such a happy and tender moment, the whole church filled with the delight of marriage and the joy of the future which lay ahead for this happy couple.

Together, they made their way arm in arm down the aisle, with much congratulating and applause. Caroline and Louis followed along behind and they emerged out into the sunshine where the birds were singing and the smell of box hedge and roses wafted on the warm summer breeze. Caroline embraced Anne once again and the two men shook hands, the two couples as happy as could be on that special day.

"Congratulations, Sir Percy. I must say that when I first met Anne she rather disliked me, but I think we have come past that now," Louis said.

Sir Percy laughed. "I was kept abreast of events by an almost constant stream of letters from London. But all is well that ended well and we are truly happy for you both," he said.

"And I have quite forgiven your earlier indiscretions," Anne said, blushing a little as she turned to Louis.

"For which I am glad. There is little worse than the closest friend of one's wife if she takes a dislike to one," Louis replied.

Anne and Caroline both laughed.

"You have nothing further to worry about, though I shall be keeping my eye on you," Anne said, wagging her finger and smiling.

"I expect nothing less," Louis replied.

"We men must stick together though, Your Grace. You and Caroline must be a regular visitor to us at my estate. We shall ride out together and the two ladies can discuss us to their heart's content," Sir Percy said.

"An excellent idea, Sir Percy. We shall be honored," Louis replied.

"Come now, we must return to Brimpton Manor. There is enough food and drink to serve the entire village and I have given the whole estate the day off in celebration of this happy occasion," Lord Brimpton called out, as he extracted himself from the crowd of well-wishers.

"Come now, Anne, we must lead the way," Sir Percy said, taking his new bride by the hand.

"Goodbye, Caroline, goodbye, Louis. We shall see you at Brimpton Manor shortly," Anne called out, waving at Caroline and Louis, as she and Sir Percy made their way to the waiting carriage.

"Ah, there you are," Richard said, hurrying up to them, "we should be getting along too."

Together, they were driven to the manor house. It seemed that the whole village had indeed descended for the celebration and the house was alive with guests. A grand feast had been laid out and there was much merrymaking and dancing already occurring when they arrived. Louis helped Caroline down from the carriage and they watched as her uncle hurried off to greet his newfound friends in the village.

"I thought he hated country life?" Louis said.

"He seems to have rather taken to it, especially after Mr. Pilkington introduced him formally to his geese," Caroline replied, laughing.

Louis took her by the arm and they walked together

onto the terrace, where several of the guests were also enjoying the midday sun.

"A splendid occasion," Louis said, as she leaned her head upon his shoulder.

"Anne's dress was simply exquisite. She looked beautiful," Caroline said.

"You looked even more so in yours. The most beautiful bride in all the world," he said, turning to her and smiling.

Caroline blushed. Their simple ceremony had been nothing compared to this. The vows pronounced in a small chapel in the city, the witnesses only their closest friends. Yet it had been the same love expressed, the same joy given, and the same happy future blessed by God. She, like Anne, had known the happiness of the man she loved, even though it had taken many years to realize it.

"Our simple ceremony was quite different. But it meant precisely the same," she replied, and he nodded, placing his arms around her.

"But how much we endured to arrive at this happy

moment. The years of separation and the pain in both our hearts. Truly it was fate which brought us together again, a marriage meant to be. Our life together will surely be more meaningful for that," he said.

Caroline laid her head upon his chest. She felt so safe and protected in his arms, just as she had done when first they had met. In the naivety of youth, she had fallen in love with him. But now in the maturity of her years, she knew that love to be as real now as it had been then. She could not imagine life without him and the years in which they had been parted seemed almost like a dream.

"And what does the future hold for us?" she asked him, looking up into his smiling face, as he leaned down to kiss her.

"A happy ending, the happiest of endings. But I think your uncle has grown rather fond of this rural backwater, as have I. I do not think you wish to return to London, do you?" he asked.

"I shall happily go wherever you go and follow you wherever you lead," she replied, and he shook his head.

"No, it is for you to lead me and I wish only to be with you," he replied.

"Then here we shall stay and we shall be the happiest of people together," Caroline replied, as he kissed her once more for the happiest of futures lay ahead of them.

To receive a free eBook and notice of my new releases, join my exclusive newsletter here. It is completely FREE to join, and you can cancel your subscription at any time.

"Now then, we really must start packing. I know we shall not be leaving until Friday, but one can never be too well prepared," Lady Ariadne Milford said as she heaved herself to her feet with her customary noisy groan. "Goodness, old age is catching up with me."

"Shall I ask the housekeeper to have your wooden trunk laid out in your room, My Lady?" Jane asked and hoped that she was being helpful. "And then, perhaps, you could tell me what you need, and I could help you pack."

"Not at all, my dear. The housekeeper has everything under control and my lady's maid will pack for me. She is well versed on my traveling needs, Jane." Lady Ariadne gave Jane a reassuring smile. "No, I think you and I shall take tea instead and discuss this nephew of mine. I daresay it will be of some use to you to know a little something of him before we arrive at Sotheby Hall." She looked across the drawing room to the bell rope hanging neatly by the side of the chimney breast. "I know it is early, my dear, but what-say you ring for tea anyway?"

"Of course, Lady Ariadne," Jane said and dutifully rose from her perch on the couch and silently hurried across the room.

"My dear, you are always so keen to help with everything." Lady Ariadne was studying Jane as she made her way back across the room. "But you really are only my companion, Jane. You must try not to be one of my servants, for you are not. I know the circumstances of your father's passing have made you nervous, but you are still a well-bred young woman. None of us know in our youth how the world is going to treat us, but we always have our breeding to fall back upon."

"You are very kind, Lady Ariadne." Jane settled back on the very edge of the couch opposite her mistress.

"Oh, do sit comfortably, Jane. You make me feel as if there is some emergency that I am not yet aware of." Lady Ariadne waved her companion back into her seat. "That's it, lean back a little at least. Is that not more comfortable?"

"Yes, thank you," Jane said and wished she could find some way to feel at her ease.

But her life had been turned upside down with the passing of her father and she felt like a fish out of water.

Her father, Lord Briars, a baron, had struggled for most of his life with a failing estate, doing everything in his power to see it continue for generations to come, even if his heir was to be his nephew. Jane had been his only child and his only relief had been to know that his nephew would have happily kept Jane safe on the estate when the time came. But when the time did come, there was nothing left for Jane's cousin to inherit and no way for that fine young man to add her to his already great responsibilities. In the end, Jane had taken matters into her own hands and struck out into the world in search of a job. Thinking first to try for a position as a governess, she had found luck at last when the very first post she had been offered had been as a companion to Lady Ariadne Milford. It was better paid and kept her status at least a bit better elevated than if she had become a governess.

"Now then, about my nephew," Lady Ariadne began, bringing Jane back into the here and now. "I have not yet told you much about him. The truth is that I did not think he would agree to see me and so I thought there was little point in giving you any of the details before now."

"I see," Jane said, not really seeing but feeling she ought to add to the conversation in some way.

It wouldn't do for her to simply smile benignly and stare out of one of Brockett Hall's ceiling-height windows or to admire the largest fireplace she had ever seen. Lady Ariadne liked her companion to be just that; a companion. She was expected to participate, to give opinions, even offer advice on occasion. But with a woman of such a forceful character as Lady Ariadne, such confidence was not easily found.

"Oh, but he was such a dear boy to me, Jane. Such a handsome little lad." Lady Ariadne looked suddenly upset and Jane, unused to dealing with such things, began to fear she had no means by which to manage. "And when he set off for Spain, his father and me pleading with him to reconsider, he was so full of enthusiasm for life and everything in it." Quite out of the blue, Lady Ariadne dabbed at her eyes with a handkerchief.

"Lady Ariadne, what is it? What is upsetting you?" Jane, feeling certain that her mistress would not want her to dash across the room and comfort her physically, decided to get to the heart of the matter.

After all, it was Lady Ariadne's way of doing things and Jane could only hope that she would appreciate a little forthrightness.

"Oh, I am upset my dear. Very upset. I am always this way when I think of my poor dear Nathaniel."

"Your nephew? But why?"

"He was so terribly wounded out there in Spain. Oh, how I wish he would never have gone."

"Lady Ariadne, forgive me, but is your nephew an invalid on account of his wounds? Is that why you are so upset?" Jane spoke gently.

"No, he is not an invalid, except that he makes himself so." Lady Ariadne, just as her character dictated, sniffed in a loud and unladylike manner without apology, forcing Jane to stifle an inappropriate laugh.

"I do not understand."

"He has made himself a recluse. That handsome boy who left home at just twenty is now a man of thirty who might just as well live in a cave for all the people he sees. He has made himself a hermit."

"And that is why you did not think he would agree to your visit?"

"Yes." Lady Ariadne blew her nose with all the grace of a farmhand. "But he has, and so I must be pleased. And I am, although I suppose it is true to say I am more relieved than anything. I have not seen him for two years. Before that it was three." She shrugged. "I just hope that he will let me help him this time. Let *us* help him," she said and looked meaningfully at Jane.

As Jane smiled kindly, she wondered just what was going to be expected of her.

"I suppose you must prepare a room for my aunt, Mrs. Marlow. It seems that she will not be denied this time." Nathaniel Alexander, the Earl of Sotheby, gave his housekeeper a defeated sigh.

"Very good, My Lord. And I shall have servants' rooms aired and ready for the lady's maid and the driver." The middle-aged housekeeper nodded slowly. "Is Lady Milford to bring anyone further, My Lord?"

"Not that I am aware of. Was that the extent of her entourage on her last visit? I can hardly remember, Mrs. Marlow."

"Yes, My Lord. Just the two servants."

"Then I suppose that is all we can prepare for." She shrugged. "My aunt is a creature of habit; I daresay she will bring the same two servants with her."

"Very well, My Lord. Will that be all?"

"Yes, thank you. I will not be needing anything else this evening," he smiled at Mrs. Marlow, letting her know she was free to get on with whatever she chose to do for the rest of the evening.

For his part, Nathaniel had already decided that a few glasses of brandy in front of the fire would serve him very nicely. He had picked out a book which he had already laid out on the side table next to his fireside armchair, although he knew he was unlikely to read a word of it.

As was common when he had something on his mind, Nathaniel would simply sit and drink by the fire with the open book on his lap and no idea of the story contained within its pages.

No sooner was the door closed than Nathaniel was on his feet approaching the drinks trolley. Even as he poured his first large serving of brandy, he could still hear the departing footsteps of Mrs. Marlow.

With a sigh, he took his glass back to the fireside and settled heavily down in the armchair, its thick blue brocade upholstery rough and pleasingly unyielding as he tried to make himself comfortable. He smiled; he liked that. Life was not easy, not even making oneself comfortable, and he did not want it to be either.

Nathaniel wanted to remind himself every day of the foolishness he had once been so guilty of. The foolishness which had made him such a bright and optimistic young man and sent him off to war all those years ago as if it was nothing more than a boy's adventure. He wanted to be reminded of his mistake every day. Not so that he never made it again, for he knew that the young man he had once been would never return. No, it was so that he could remind himself exactly who was to blame for his current life; the life which would be his until he was finally tipped into the grave.

The scars which covered his right upper body and part of his face had been his doing. His self-imposed exile from the world had been his doing. His loneliness had been his doing.

It seemed to Nathaniel that even his loneliness was not enough to make him truly want the company of his aunt, nor anybody else. The only people he could bear to see were his staff, and only because they were so used to his appearance that they never gave any indication that something was amiss.

They had at first, of course, but how could they not have? He had left Sotheby Hall as a handsome man of twenty with all the arrogance of youth. He had returned a very different man just two years later, a man who would bear the scars of his foolhardy youth for the rest of his life.

The staff at Sotheby had, by nothing more than familiarity, grown used to their master as he was now, and it had been a relief to him that his beloved father had passed before he had returned from the war.

It had broken his heart, for Nathaniel had loved his father, but he loved him so much that he could not have suffered to see the effect his altered appearance would have had on him. His aunt's devastation had been more than enough.

Still, Lady Ariadne was a tough old soul and she was much better able to hide her sadness these days, even if she could not hide it completely. It was not as if she was going to be seeing him afresh; she would not gape at him the way strangers or even acquaintances did whenever he chanced to leave the walls and grounds of Sotheby.

"Oh, perhaps I will enjoy the company," he said to himself rather loudly before gulping down every drop of brandy in the glass. "Perhaps this visit will be a good thing."

He leaned back in his armchair, feeling the rough brocade beneath his flattened palm, and stared into the flames.

Nathaniel knew, of course, that his beloved aunt could not help but try to find some way to help him. He knew she could not bear the idea of his self-determined seclusion and would try everything in her power to drag him out into the world again.

She was a strong old thing and she certainly took some fending off. Nathaniel shook his head and realized he was smiling; not a thing he did very often.

Perhaps it was time to let her in just a little, she loved him dearly after all.

"Perhaps," he said to himself again as he rose to pour himself another brandy. "Perhaps."

Read The Dance of Love for FREE with Kindle Unlimited

And many more...

To find all of Charlotte's books, Follow her on <u>Amazon</u>. Just click the yellow follow button when you get to Amazon and they will send you details of special offers and new releases.

I hope you enjoyed these books by Charlotte Darcy.

Charlotte is a hopeless romantic. She loves historical romance and the Regency era the most. She has been a writer for many years and can think of nothing better than seeing how her characters can find their happy ever after.

She lives in Derbyshire, England and when not writing you will find her walking the British countryside with her dog Poppy or visiting stately homes, such as Chatsworth House which is local to her.

You can contact Charlotte at CharlotteDarcy@cd2.com or via Facebook at @CharlotteDarcyAuthor

Or join my exclusive newsletter for a free book and updates on new releases here.

www.ingramcontent.com/pod-product-compliance
Lightning Source LLC
Chambersburg PA
CBHW021206130726
47988CB00002B/531